UNUSUAL SUSPECTS

Four Stories of Suspicion Suspense and Murder

S Paul Klein

PEAK PRESS

HEAD WATERS, VA

To my GREAT. WRITING LEADER!

Paul Klein

Other writers praise S Paul Klein's novel, *Accidents of Time and Place*

Accidents of Time and Place gives the reader a tense view of individuals caught in Washington conspiracy phobia. Many of us have suppressed recall of this era. Klein brings it back to life with chilling immediacy.

William Crisp - Author of **Goodbye Vienna**

In **Accidents of Time and Place**, Paul Klein paints a profound and insightful picture of a sleepy Washington DC, and an introverted, wounded war hero who takes up his life as an older student after years of war and service to his country. Hector Collin's travel from coal mine to army hero to older student and eventual writer is a poignant and smoothly delivered story, with extremely likable and well developed characters and an appealing and uplifting plot.

Jean C. Keating - National award winning author of **Beguiling Bundle**

Very smoothly written novel. The descriptions of 1950's are positively lyrical! Klein has captured the 'time and place' perfectly. Very deep, convincing, well-drawn characters. A pleasant and inspiring story, without jumps or contrivances.

Ann Babcock - Author of **Waiting For Permission** and **Nest Of The Walking Wounded**

ISBN:-10: 0615956475
ISBN-13: 978-0615956473

:

DEDICATION

These stories are dedicated to the memory of the man behind Badge 35. A warrior's life well lived has earned him his rest.

.

Contents

ACKNOWLEDGMENTS

There are certain people who contribute knowingly to a writer's work. Foremost among them are the members of the Highland Writer's Group, who have read and helped refine and encourage the completion of these stories. A special thanks to "Eagle Eye" Mike, who sees all. There is a police officer behind badge 114, whose knowledge of procedure, protocol and the ways of her world has at least tried to make my imagined world a real one. And of course, First Reader, who always encourages what I do with expert commentary delivered with love, is the one I write for.

A Beautiful Place For An Ugly Death

There are places where everyone knows everyone, where nothing is hidden, unless you are a stranger. Then you will learn nothing, find no one, unless you look elsewhere. It can be a beautiful place.

WHITECHAPEL, VIRGINIA

IN THE OLD GREEN AND WHITE PICKUP, Don Jackson fit the profile of a mountain man: long-legged, strong arms, a frame that easily carried his 200 pounds. Though the evening had cooled, he drove with the window open, the heavy flannel shirt and beat-up feedstore cap providing all the protection he needed from the chilled air. Jackson smiled as he rounded the last turn at the bottom of the mountain. Two miles more and he would turn off the highway. Away from it all. Away from everything. Away from her.

Over the bridge, wide enough for logging trucks to make the turn leading up the next mountain, Jackson swung a hard right onto the gravel road. High mountain on one side, flat bottomland on the other. He drove the last five-hundred yards to the steel gate slowly, not reluctantly, but to increase his pleasure at arriving at Riversee. She had named it in the clever way she had with words. It grated on

7

him, so he never pronounced it. To him it was just "the cabin."

On his own lane now, he continued to roll slowly until he had to accelerate slightly up the incline leading to the bridge over the narrow river. The previous owner had been an engineer, and the bridge was every bit as strong and as permanent as a highway crossing. A wide concrete abutment on either side of the river carried steel I-beams. Oak planking, stained dark with oil to protect it, made a chattering noise as the tires of the pick-up rolled across. A rapid, rhythmic, "good-good-good-good" was how Don heard the sound as he crossed the bridge.

THE SUN THAT WAS JUST LEAVING THE MOUNTAIN TOWN of Whitechapel had dropped from the Washington skyline nearly half-an-hour earlier. In the downtown apartment on Pennsylvania Avenue, near the old post office, Adrienne Jackson glanced at the gold and onyx clock on the mantle of the black marble fireplace in the study. Don would be at Riversee by now, she thought. *God! I hate that old cabin, and he can't live without it. What a waste.* She nodded her head, agreeing with herself.

Picking up a sheaf of papers from the desk, she crossed the room and sat down by the fireplace. They seldom used it, but it made the study seem cozy, and tonight she was feeling very much in need of cozy. Standing, she picked up a butane lighter from the table. Kneeling easily, brushing her long, thick hair over one shoulder, she spread the fire screen, opened the damper, and ignited the fire-starter set beneath the three manufactured logs. How civilized, she thought. No wadding paper, no sticks and very little mess when the fire had burned itself out. Settled in her chair, the papers in her lap, she watched the dancing flames. So easy. Easy. Not like the "back-to-nature" stone fireplace at Riversee. The dust, the effort of rolling up papers ("six to eight, no more," Don cautioned), breaking the twigs and branches into kindling (never mind the flecks and flakes of bark and splinters on the riverjack hearth), then three logs stacked so that they made a shape like an A-frame house. And more flecks and flakes and then ashes. And it all had to be cleaned out before going home. Well, at least he always took care of that when they were there together. Which wasn't very often now. *And*, Adrienne realized with some impatience, *he doesn't seem to mind!*

THE FIREPLACE IN THE LIVING ROOM wasn't for looks in this house, Don mused. Big stones, carefully placed long ago by some local craftsman, a hearth of smaller rock taken from the river, and a stone chimney that penetrated the ceiling and roof. The house was at least a century old, made of twelve-inch logs. In the 1930s rough-sawn planks had been placed vertically board-on-board to cover the outside. Smooth, hand-planed tongue-and-groove boards set horizontally clad the inside. Three rooms had been enough for the first owner, with two rooms up a narrow stair set in the middle of the single downstairs room. Don had bought the farm in the 80s, paying what then was an exorbitant $500 an acre for the 70 acres on both sides of the river. A creek really, but locally known as "the river."

With a fresh fire burning hard, Don sat down on the leather sofa facing the hearth. He kicked off the moccasins he usually wore indoors and settled back, letting the fire cut the chill of the October night. Outside the temperature was already at 43 degrees, and would go lower before sunrise. *Frost in the morning*, Don mused. He watched the flames, and planned his early morning hike into the woods. "Turkeys look out," he said to the flames. "Look out." He closed his eyes and drifted into a pleasant preview of the hunting season ahead.

WASHINGTON, D.C.

THE FIRE IN THE FIREPLACE ON PENNSYLVANIA AVENUE elicited anything but turkeys in Adrienne's thoughts. She was thinking about Riversee, though. Don loved the outdoors, and much of their early courtship was spent walking in the woods of Rock Creek Park, the long greenway that cut through the city from Maryland before spilling into the Potomac. Not the kind of hell-for-leather hikes Teddy Roosevelt had led, but civilized, hand-in-hand rambles along well-tended paths.

They had dated off-and-on for nearly a year before he took her to the cabin the first time. It was late in the Fall, and the first snow had already been on the ground for a week. She was charmed by the long drive through the Virginia countryside, and the twisty mountain road that swept up and back until it breached the top, then wiggled its way down into the village.

WHEN THEY MARRIED, IT WAS A LATE FIRST MARRIAGE for both of them: two professionals pursuing careers of high caliber and stress. Weekends at the cabin were always romantic, delivering equal measures of tranquility and powerful release. Adrienne had especially looked forward to the Spring, when the trees began to leaf-out against a background of fresh snow despite the warming sunny days. They had been married in March, and honeymooned at the cabin. They had loved and laughed and spent the days walking the woods or along the river. Don had introduced her to the simple pleasure of fishing, teaching her to identify native and brown trout that hid beneath the limestone shelves or tree roots that extended from the banks. She found the tranquility restful and the skill a challenge.

As the summer ended, Don began to talk about hunting. He wanted to take a day or two in November when turkey season opened, and then maybe another week later, during deer season. The idea of her man hunting to feed them appealed to some atavism in her character. She accompanied him on both trips, and was rewarded, between seasons, with a shotgun of her own. Surprised, too; surprise at her own instinctive sureness with the weapon. Don called her a natural. Her eyes could discern a target, even a small one, and with only a simple demonstration, she had understood and mastered leading a moving target. If she saw what she wanted to shoot, it was as good as dead.

NORTHERN VIRGINIA

"IS MR. JACKSON IN HIS OFFICE?" Sam Hamilton, in his usual blue oxford cloth, button-down shirt and tweed jacket, stood in the doorway of the office. Serena Lorenz looked up from her computer

"No, Mr. Hamilton, he hasn't come back yet."

"I thought he had finished that job a week ago. I had heard he was back on Thursday."

"Yes, that's right. But he was going away for the weekend. He might have gotten a late start this morning."

"Well, let me know as soon as he gets in. I have some questions about what happened over there." Hamilton turned and let the door swing closed.

When Don Jackson hadn't come in by noon, Serena placed a call to his home. No answer. There was no telephone at the cabin, she knew, and it was located in a cell phone dead zone, so when that number went unanswered, she wasn't surprised. After half an hour her phone rang, but it was not Jackson.

"Grady," a voice identified itself brusquely. "Jackson still missing?"

11

"I don't know that he's missing, Mr. Grady. He was taking a long weekend off. He has a lot of time coming, after his last assignment."

"Missing," Grady insisted. "I'll put things in motion."

This was not an office where tardy employees were simply marked "late" and put out of mind. There were people whose job it was to put the worst-case complexion on any variation in routine or act. Grady, because of Don Jackson's high level status, would take on the task of looking for him.

Hamilton and Grady were reviewing Jackson's trip report on a secure screen. According to the log and narrative, Don had slipped into and out of the east-European capital with remarkable ease. No customs or immigration questions, no secret service interviews, just a normal American businessman visiting a potential new market. His meetings with his contacts, in the shadow of the city's central mosque, had been quick, not threatening, and over in a short time. Don had spent two days in the city, reported no breech of his hotel room while he was out of it, and no difficultly leaving the country.

"Very smooth operation," Hamilton mused.

"Too smooth, maybe." Grady wasn't often willing to accept what he could see.

WHITECHAPEL, VIRGINIA

WHAT HE COULDN'T SEE was that Don Jackson was dead. He lay face down in the leaves. This was rocky soil, very thin, and trees fought for their place by sending roots out, over and around rocks that got in the way. Part of his face was still there. The right half of it was scattered on the leaves and trees beside the trail. His right hand still clutched a 20-gauge shotgun by the receiver, his finger near the trigger guard, the barrel pointing toward his head. The trail was tending downhill, and the toe of Don's left boot seemed caught in a tree root that crossed the surface of the trail. Animals both large and small had been over the ground by the time the sun cut through the early morning mist, but the frost had slowed the effect the sun would have later. There was a lot to see, for someone who knew how to look.

Two hunters, cutting across Jackson's land from the national forest, were the first to see him there. It was obvious that he was dead, and it was also obvious that they were trespassing. Instead of continuing across the posted land, they turned and quickly retraced their steps into the forest. As quickly as they could they used a public access trail to return to their truck. Turning it around, they headed out to the main highway, and a pay phone across from the country store.

The older man lifted the receiver from the hook and heard a dial tone. His forefinger stabbed the 9 and the 1 and the 1 again. There was the sound of a connection and then a click. "County Sheriff's Office. This is Sandy. What is your emergency?" The calm voice helped the man get his thoughts in order.

"I'm at the phone booth across from the Whitechapel Store."

"Yessir?"

"There's been an accident."

"Yessir. Can you tell me where?"

"In the -- in the woods near the access trail on Little Fork."

"Can you tell me what happened?"

13

"I don't know. We were coming along the trail and we found this man lying there. He's been shot."

"Ok, sir. Please stay on the line. Can you tell me exactly where the accident happened?"

"Just off the access trail. Near where it crosses the land of that place called 'Riversee.'"

"Can you describe the injury, sir?"

"The man is dead. Head's all bloody. That's all I know."

"Please stay on the line, sir," but the man had already placed the receiver back on the hook.

Across the highway the storekeeper watched the two men as they crowded the phone booth. They were familiar to him, as were most of the men who hunted in the woods around the village. Before getting back in the truck, the two men walked across and came into the store.

"How ya doin," the storekeeper asked in his laconic drawl, stepping toward the counter from the wall he had been leaning against.

"Cold," said the younger man. "Not this cold in Pennsylvania, yet."

"Well," the storeman said, "likely be colder tonight."

"Guess we're going home," the older of the two said.

Paying for a couple of beers and ready-made sandwiches, the two didn't linger, but crossed the road, got back in the truck, and headed east, out of the county.

It wasn't long before a tan patrol car pulled up in front of the pumps. The deputy said something on his radio, and then got out of the car and came into the store.

Again the storekeeper moved forward to the counter. This time he took the stool behind the register as his resting place. The deputy, David Smith, paused in the doorway, looking around the narrow, dimly lit store. The only people he could see were Jacob and his wife Darlene, the postmistress. Darlene was at the back of the store still sorting the morning mail.

"Hey David," Jacob said slowly.

"Hey, Jacob. Anybody else in the store?"

Jacob looked around. "Who ya'll lookin' for?"

"Don't know. Had a 9-1-1 call about twenty minutes ago, from the pay phone."

"Yeah, I did see two fellas using it. Came in here for a minute, then said they were headin' home. Said it was too cold for 'em."

"Know who they were?"

"Naw. Seen 'em before, though. Come from up in Pennsylvania somewhere."

A tenth of a mile west, where the gravel road began, a line of cars was already heading to Don Jackson's gate. In the lead was the sheriff's Ford Expedition, followed closely by a silver and blue state police cruiser. The gate at Riversee was open, as it always was when Don was there. The vehicles pulled up in front of the cabin, next to the pickup truck with DC license plates. For a moment the occupants remained in their cars, then the sheriff opened the door of his Expedition and got out. Slowly he walked to the steps, calling out in a loud voice, "Mr. Jackson, you there?"

15

The state trooper joined him at the steps, and the two men walked up to the door.

"Try the door, Bert," Trooper Haines suggested. The door opened without resistance. It was immediately obvious that the main room was empty. "Ashes in the fireplace are cold," Haines said, sifting them with a poker. "Let's go up the trail behind the house."

The men walked around the cabin and picked up a trail that led into the woods. Walking carefully, they began the ascent up the back of Shenandoah Mountain. Less than 500 yards from the cabin they found the scene that the anonymous caller had described.

WASHINGTON, D.C.

AT TEN O'CLOCK, ADRIENNE JACKSON WAS JUST BEGINNING HER LECTURE on legal aspects of international trade compacts. Near her, on the lecture platform, her graduate assistant managed the slide changes on the lap-top connected to the video projector. Jason Arno was only a few years younger than Adrienne, only a little taller, with Nordic blonde hair and dark, almost black eyes.

The professor was just concluding her general observations on the subject when Grady appeared at the door. Stepping into the room, he let the door close softly behind him. When Adrienne saw him her voice faltered momentarily. It was nothing about his appearance that startled her. It was his being there at all. Without changing the tone of her delivery, she paused, then said, "Excuse me. I must interrupt for a moment. Mr. Arno," she turned to her graduate assistant, "please distribute the lecture outline while I step out of the room."

Arno left the computer table and picked up the outline sheets from a small table beside the lectern. After he handed them to

16

the student nearest the podium, he stood and watched the professor walk purposefully from the room. The door closed silently behind her.

At the doorway she looked at Grady a second before saying, "What's happened?"

"I've just had a call from the local sheriff down in Whitechapel," Grady said quietly. "They think Don's had an accident."

"Oh! Where is he? How bad? What happened?" Her words came quickly, but her voice never rose above little more than a whisper.

"An accident in the woods." Grady's voice was low, matter-of-fact. "I'm afraid he's been shot."

Adrienne paled visibly. Putting out a hand she grasped Grady's arm. "By whom? Why are you involved?"

"We don't know anything much yet. A couple of hunters reported finding him a few hours ago. The state police called me because they know Don's connection to us. We're on our way down there now."

Adrienne looked down at her shoes. She looked up into Grady's eyes. They told her nothing. Neither could he read anything in hers. "I - I must get back to my class."

"Do you want to come with us?" Grady was prepared to add her to the jet waiting at Andrews Air Force Base just across the Anacostia. "We're going to meet the state police in Roanoke and then go to Whitechapel."

"No" the woman answered softly. "What hospital is he in?"

"I'm sorry, Adrienne. Don's dead." There was no nice way to say it, Grady knew, and the longer he waited to do it, the harder it would be. He studied the woman. She seemed as cool and professional as if she were simply an acquaintance of the dead man. "Is your office near here?" He waived his hand to indicate the corridor. "Maybe we should go there. Is there someone I can call?" he said, almost as an afterthought. Grady wasn't as comfortable delivering emotional support as he was bringing bad news.

Shaking her head, she looked down the hall, then at her classroom door. Without a word she opened the door and stepped back inside. *Her safety zone*, Grady mused as he turned and left the building.

Cool and stoic, Adrienne walked to the lecture platform and announced that she would have to conclude the lecture immediately. Admonishing the students to digest the outline they had been given, she turned to her assistant. "Come to the office as soon as you close the room." Stepping off the platform, she again left the room. Down the corridor and to the left she opened the door to her office, and walked in. Walking through the anteroom where her assistant worked, she entered her own private sanctuary. She stood looking out the window for a minute or two, her eyes closed to the view of the quadrangle below.

"What is it, Adrienne?" Jason came in without knocking, demonstrating a familiarity Adrienne found only momentarily disconcerting.

Turning, she looked directly in Jason's black eyes. "Don is dead," she said flatly. Her face was blank, her eyes dry. Jason stepped forward and put his arms around her. In his embrace Adrienne seemed small, though she was nearly as tall as he. She relaxed a little, putting her arms around him, and rested her cheek against his shoulder. A somber moment seemed to pass, before she

18

raised her face to his. Her hands pulled his head toward her. Their lips met. She clung to him for just a moment. Stepping back, the woman looked again into the man's eyes.

"Thank you," she said quietly. "We must be careful now, Jason. There will be a lot of eyes looking at us. You understand?"

The man nodded his head. His eyes held hers. "I'll try to be good," he whispered. Pressing her to him once more, he held her, then let her go.

WHITE CHAPEL, VIRGINIA

FROM HIS CRUISER, Trooper Haines had contacted his headquarters in Salem. Now a black helicopter was overhead, while the chief from the local volunteer fire department talked the pilot down in the field a mile south of the cabin.

"Find the windsock to the west of the paved road," the chief said. "Tall grass and no rocks in the field."

"10-4, Chief 2. We have you in sight. Coming in Northwest."

SHERIFF BERTRAND STOOD BESIDE THE BODY. Looking back down the trail he was surprised to see two men and a woman approaching the scene. One of the men he recognized. The other and the woman were new to him. *Must be from Richmond,* he speculated. As they walked up, Lieutenant Morris stuck out his hand and greeted Bertrand.

"Hello, Bert. Been a long time." Looking down at the body, he commented, "Got something interesting, I see."

"Maybe," the sheriff said. "Didn't think it would be as

19

interesting as all this," indicating the two strangers, "Richmond interested?"

"Washington," said Grady. "He worked for us."

Bert looked at the squat, colorless man in the gray civil service suit: "Who's 'us'?"

"Mr. Grady is with a government agency," Morris answered.

"Let's get started." The government man's voice was impatient.

"Who's in charge, Lieutenant?" the sheriff asked. "Me, you, them?" He nodded at Grady and his companion.

"Depends on what we find, Sheriff," Grady rumbled. A short, round man, he stood with his feet together, giving the impression of a very old, very fixed boulder.

Standing around the body, now covered with a sheet from the funeral home vehicle, Bertrand summed up what they had found: "I'd say you probably have an accidental discharge, caused by a stumble. His foot is caught by the root, the wound to the head is consistent with a shotgun fired close and upward, and the marks on the remaining skin look right for powder burns."

A short silence followed, and then Grady growled into the discussion.

"Could be, Sheriff, but maybe not. I'd like some forensic work before the body is moved."

The sheriff and the state men looked at each other. Their thoughts were transparent: *Here go the Feds, making work for themselves and us!*

Grady looked at his watch. "Should be a team here in a few minutes," he said. "I turned 'em on before we left. Meantime, Agent King will be in charge of this." He nodded to his colleague. "Stay with it, Lissa, and keep me in the picture." He turned toward the cabin. "And keep everybody out of the house," he said over his shoulder. His city shoes were slippery on the leaves, and he walked carefully down the trail.

"Well, Ms. King," Morris said, "I guess it's your party." Then he turned and started to follow Grady back to the vehicles.

"Lieutenant," her voice was authoritative but not abrasive, "can you stay here while I see Mr. Grady for a few minutes? Our team will take over as soon as they get here." Morris nodded, and the young woman followed the others down the trail.

"Now isn't that just terrific," Haines said.

The Sheriff, who had been standing close to the trees, smiled and looked after the group now almost out of sight. "Suits me, Haines. Any mistakes get made, let them make 'em. Saves a lot of paperwork on my part, too." Then he followed the others.

Kneeling beside the body, Morris pulled the sheet back from the head and shoulders. Staring at the mutilated face, he followed a line back to the gun barrel. "Interesting," was all he said to Haines.

IT WAS NEARLY AFTERNOON before the hearse drove out of the yard. Instead of turning west on the main highway, the driver turned east, and settled back for the two-hour drive to Roanoke and the state medical examiner's office. The federal team had released the body, and armed with photographs, soil samples, and other evidence, all in plastic or brown paper bags, all sealed and marked, they descended on the cabin. Yellow "crime scene" tape was wrapped around the whole building, put there by one of Sheriff Bertrand's deputies.

"Probably the first time they've had to use it," one of the agents laughed.

"Don't cut these boys too short," his companion said. "I spent a couple of years in a county force back in Iowa, before I joined the office. We had our share, and we took it just as seriously as you do."

The older man regarded the other briefly, then ducked under the tape.

THE SLANTING SUN coming through the window cast Lissa King's shadow across the floor, backlighting her golden hair and accentuating her tall, trim figure. She stood to one side as her colleagues sifted the ashes in the fireplace. The light also caught the swirl of ash, defining the shaft of light even more. From the other side of the room, Lieutenant Morris watched not the process, but Agent King.

"Your first time in these hills?" he said, when Lissa looked from the fireplace to him.

"No. In fact," she smiled, "I was part of a team that checked the security here a year ago."

"Did you think something was going on?"

"No, just a routine thing we do for some of our people. If nobody knows about this place, security is easy. But if it's common knowledge, well," she glanced around the room, "that makes it almost impossible. We don't have the resources to cover a place like this full-time."

Morris turned and looked out the window behind him. "I see what you mean," he said, nodding toward the road. A few pickups and a van had gathered along the road, and a few people, some in hunting cammo and others in jeans and windbreakers, stood around the open gate. Trooper Haines and the deputy from the sheriff's office stood inside the gate, obviously being questioned by the people on the other side.

"I wonder what you could learn if you were down there listening to what they're saying," King suggested. "Might pick up a vibe or two."

"I could do that," he agreed, stepping toward the door.

"If you know these people, you might notice a stranger faster than I would," Lissa added.

Morris walked outside, let his eyes adjust to the brightness, and then went slowly down the path to the gate a hundred yards away. Now it was King's turn to watch as the man moved to his task. She estimated Morris to be about forty, recognized the easy movement of a natural athlete, mentally subtracted 20 pounds added by time and hours spent in the tedious tasks of an investigators life, and (though she wasn't aware of it) approved of her temporary partner.

Turning back to the two agents at the fireplace, she readjusted her focus and asked if there was anything in the cold fireplace.

"Just some heat in the stones," said the younger man, holding a thermal imager. "I'd guess the fire was burning when our guy left the house, say about eight hours ago."

"Otherwise, nothing." The other agent stood up slowly and looked around. "We've already gone over the upstairs rooms. Didn't look as if he slept up there last night." Inclining his head toward the leather sofa, he added, "I'd say he spent the night right here in front of the fire."

"Any sign of another person?" Lissa asked.

"Nope. We even looked for a second glass or plate that had been recently washed, you know, like somebody cleaning up after themselves." The agent shook his head. "No happiness there, either."

"What about his gun cabinet? Did you open it?"

"Yes, ma'am. Only one other gun in it, and that's a .30-.30 with a scope." The older agent picked up the keys and unlocked the cabinet again. "Space for a couple of more, of course, but that doesn't mean there are any missing."

Lissa walked to the open cabinet and looked in. Pulling a small LED flashlight from her shoulder bag, she bent and examined the felt on the part of the rack where the butt-plate of a gun would rest. "A little wear on more than one place," she said half aloud. "I wonder." Her voice trailed off. Standing, she turned to the two men and held out her hand. "Let me have the keys. I think we can lock up, but I may want to come back tomorrow."

MOUNT ROYAL, VIRGINIA

LISSA'S OFFICE HAD FOUND A B&B just on the edge of Mount Royal, about half a mile west of the courthouse. It was an old Victorian farmhouse, two stories of white-painted wood siding with a red standing-seam metal roof, A generous porch ran along the west side, and the fields ran out and up the mountainside. A sign beside the door proclaimed that the farm had been continuously operated by the same family for more than a hundred years. The antiques that filled the rooms were as well tended as the house and the farm itself.

In her bedroom Lissa sat on the edge of the spindle bed and

looked through her notes. If she left everything and went back to Washington, she could probably close the file and let the state pursue its line of a hunting accident, certainly. But she really needed to be a part of this investigation. Maybe it wouldn't be as open and shut as it seemed. Yes, the shotgun Don carried had been discharged, and yes the wound was consistent with weapon, but how would a man as experienced as Jackson let that kind of accident happen? Would that state police detective look at that? As she re-read her notes, she heard footsteps coming up the narrow stairway.

"Ms. King?" She heard her hostess call her name.

"Yes?"

"There's a state trooper downstairs to see you."

Lissa put down her notes and stood up. She hadn't done more than take off her boots before sitting down, so she went to the door noticing the coolness of the floor against her bare feet.

Opening the door she found the pleasant older woman about to turn back down the stairs. "Please tell him I'll be right down." Funny how formal the people in this part of the world were. It had taken the young woman only an hour of exposure to realize that the easy informality of the city had not yet reached this remote outpost. Slipping into low-healed shoes, Lissa left her room and went down the stairs to meet her "gentleman caller."

She was surprised and pleased to see Stan Morris standing in the front parlor.

"Here she is," her hostess said, as if handing off a daughter to her prom date.

"I hope you don't mind my calling at this hour," Morris offered. "I thought you might be working on your report and I could help."

The older woman smiled at what sounded to her like a teenager using homework as an excuse to call on a young girl. *Don't have to be a detective to figure that out.* "You can use the dining room table if you'd like. William and I are off to bed," she said as she left the room.

Lissa smiled at the retreating figure. "I'll just get my notes," she said, and went quickly back up the stairs. Her hand smoothed her hair as she glanced in the tall mirror that stood near the door.

Sitting at the old and solid oak table, he at the end, and she to his right, they began discussing their work. Lissa felt a strong pull toward this somewhat distant man beside her . . . a pull, and potentially a problem. His competence as an investigator emerged in the questions he asked, and the way in which he listened to her ideas. But there was something in him that raised a warning. His questions were legitimate and to the point, she realized. Was there something else? Her instincts told her he was just doing his job. Was there more to it than that?

"What's your real interest in this, Lieutenant?"

"Maybe just my nature. To be suspicious I mean. Maybe I just don't believe in either accidents or perfect crimes."

I know how I want this story to end. How can I use his obvious interest to make that happen?

"We'll just have to follow this to the end, then, won't we?"

WHEN LISSA STEPPED OUTSIDE, FINE SNOW CRYSTALS were drifting down across the morning sun, evaporating before they touched the ground. The air itself was crisp and dry, a perfect Fall morning in the mountains.

Lieutenant Morris opened the door of his unmarked car and stepped out into the sunshine too. "Good morning," he called to Lissa. "I know you wanted to spend some time at the scene this morning. I do, too. Figured I'd offer you a ride."

Her hand shielding her eyes from the bright sun also covered the momentary dark look in her eyes. Lissa stepped off the front porch and let the warming sun capture her. The light caused a shimmering effect around her blonde hair. "It's so beautiful here. It's like fifty years ago."

"Last time I had anything to do here was a missing person from Virginia Beach," Stan said. "It was my first assignment when I joined the State Police. Things haven't changed much since then."

Lissa opened the passenger door and got in. Stan looked at her, absorbing the silhouette created by the morning sun. He smiled, then turned away.

"How long ago was that?"

"About fifteen years."

Interesting. He looks older than that. I wonder what he was doing before? "Was Sheriff Bertrand here then?"

"Yep. He hasn't changed much, either. A good man. Solid. Lets his deputies do their job."

They were passing the courthouse. Its white columns and Greek Revival style complimented the one- and two-storey homes and commercial buildings that filled in around it on Main Street. "That's the sheriff's office, there." Stan pointed to the building just to the left of the courthouse. "Jail too, but I don't think they use it any longer."

"No bad boys, here?"

"Not enough to justify a jail, at any rate. No, they set up a regional jail in the next county over."

As they rolled down the street, Lissa looked at the shops, but without much interest. She wasn't a shopper.

"Have you had breakfast?"

"Yes," Lissa nodded.

"I haven't. If you don't mind, we can stop here." He pulled to the curb in front of a restaurant. The sign boasted that this was the place for "home cooking."

"I can always have another cup of coffee."

The restaurant was long and narrow, with old-fashioned booths on either side. Generations of locals and visitors had carved names and initials into the wooden walls and benches. Some of the names dated back half a century. Lissa smiled as she read the inscriptions. "They must be doing something right," she ventured, "if the place hasn't changed since 1950." She pointed to initials and a date just below the chrome sconce lamp affixed to the wall.

Part of one side of the room was given over to a counter with red plastic covered stools, and a marble-topped soda fountain. A sign above the mirror on the wall advertised ice cream, milk shakes and sodas, "The kind made with ice cream and soda water," Morris pointed out. "I bet they still make 'em if you know enough to ask."

When they had ordered, Lissa looked around the room. The booths were mostly empty, but the tables that filled the center of the room were occupied by groups of five or six people, mostly men in overalls, jeans, Carhart jackets and feed store caps. The two investigators had hardly caused a raised eyebrow when they had entered.

"I imagine they will be talking about us as soon as we leave," Lissa said, her eyes on the table nearest the cash register.

"Oh, they know who we are, rest assured."

"Sure they do." It was Sheriff Bertrand. Morris looked up, then slid over to make room for him. "Thank you," Bert said, but instead put his hands palm down on the table and bent forward. "Got some place to be this morning?"

Lissa nodded. "Going back to the scene. There are some things I want to look at before I leave for Washington."

"Won't find any more bodies, I hope." He smiled. "Well, if I can be of help, let me know, Stan." He turned to Morris and smiled. Inclining his head toward the rear table, he added in a lower tone, "I'll see what the 'liar's table' has to make of it myself. Might have the answer already." He smiled, straightened up and went to the back table.

WHITECHAPEL, VIRGINIA

AS THEY CROSSED EACH OF THE THREE MOUNTAINS between the county seat and the village near Riversee, Lissa let her thoughts follow the steep and ragged peaks, the deep and misty valleys, and the smooth but twisty road that carried them east. When they pulled up to the cabin she sat for a moment before opening her door.

"A beautiful place for an ugly death." She got out and stood looking around.

Using the keys, she opened the cabin and walked in. Lieutenant Morris offered to look around the outbuildings, and she gave him the keys before turning her attention to the interior.

She opened the gun cabinet and examined the inside again, letting her mind absorb the texture of the felt, the smell of gun oil and gunpowder solvent. She ran her fingers over the indentations at the bottom where the guns rested. Closing the door, she looked speculatively at the cabinet, letting her hand slide over the softly waxed wood. Nodding her head, as if saying "yes" to herself, she turned and walked to the kitchen counter. Through the window over the sink she could see Lieutenant Morris go from the first of two outbuildings to the second one. She watched him for a few seconds, enjoying (she realized) looking at him. He was a man who moved with easy grace, even over the rocky and uneven ground in front of the buildings. She consciously moved her thoughts back to the reason she was here. Unlocking and opening the back door, she went out to join him.

Hearing her coming, Morris turned and nodded to the building he had just left.

"If you like old tractors, you can see a beauty in there. My guess is he only used it a few times a year."

Lissa looked in the open door. A gray tractor with red wheels and black seat was parked precisely in the middle of the garage. A few implements, most of which she didn't recognize, were neatly parked or hung on the walls around the tractor. The building was otherwise unremarkable, except, she thought, that is was so clean. Don had been a very careful person, she thought, and that made an accidental death seem very unlikely.

Stepping away from the tractor building, she joined Morris in the next one. Like the garage, it was built of dark-stained pine boards, nailed horizontally and overlapping. This building had windows in the side walls, and a single door on the front. Inside was a clean, neat but well used workbench, closed cabinets above and shelves below. On the opposite wall another set of shelves held reels of fishing line, a collection of reels and the small bits and pieces that every fisherman collects over time. A glass-fronted cabinet held a collection of fly rods and spinning rods to go with the reels and line. A worn fishing vest hung on a hook near the door.

Morris stood beside King and looked about him. Neither moved for a minute or more. Finally it was Morris who spoke.

"Your man must have been a really controlled guy."

Lissa looked up at him. "Why?"

"Do you fish?"

"No. It's pretty much a mystery to me."

"Well, the only guys I know who are this neat don't enjoy fishing that much. But this fellow has enough gear to outfit a small store, and it isn't just for show. Its been used a lot. He must have spent a lot of his time here cleaning and putting things away."

"Part of the training," Lissa suggested. "Never leave things disordered or disorganized. That way you can tell if someone has been looking at your stuff."

The Lieutenant looked at the federal agent for a moment. "Exactly what did this man do?"

"I thought you knew better than to ask." The woman turned to look back to the cabin, as a vehicle came crunching up the gravel drive.

Adrienne parked beside the black unmarked car. Befitting a widow, her jeans, turtleneck, leather jacket and boots were black. Getting out of the SUV, she stood for a moment looking around.

The yellow crime scene tape was still around the cabin. Turning, she looked up the gravel roadway and saw a man and a woman in the doorway of the workshop. They were looking at her with as much interest as she was looking at them. She didn't know many of the people in Don's agency, but she recognized Lissa. The annual security inspections had introduced her to the young woman. Her impression then had been that agent King was much more intelligent than she seemed. The man beside her was a complete stranger.

King and Morris met Adrienne half way between the cabin and the shop. "Hello Mrs. Jackson," She put out her hand. "I'm sorry to see you again under these circumstances."

"Agent King, isn't it?" Adrienne took the proffered hand in hers. She looked at King's companion.

"This is Lieutenant Morris, Virginia State Police. We're investigating the" she hesitated, "the accident jointly."

"How do you do?"

"As agent King said, Mrs. Jackson, sorry to meet under these circumstances. My condolences."

"Thank you. I'm afraid I'm still a bit in shock over the whole thing."

"Understandable," Morris said. Adrienne turned her head slightly to better see King's face. She couldn't read the other's expression, but Lissa sensed a sudden withdrawal in Adrienne. "Protective" was the word that popped into her mind.

"Your Mr. Grady . . ." Adrienne began, paused, began again, ". . . your Mr. Grady said it was an accident. Why are you here?" She looked at Lissa and then at Stan.

Lissa's voice was without emotion when she responded: "Our rule, Mrs. Jackson, is that when anything happens to one of our people, we treat it as suspicious until we prove it otherwise."

"What does this have to do with the state police?" Adrienne turned to Morris.

"It's our turf, Mrs. Jackson. So we want to be involved from the beginning, if we can."

"Well," was all Adrienne could offer. Turning, she started for the cabin. Morris and King looked at each other, and then followed.

"Did you want to go into the cabin, Mrs. Jackson?" Lissa asked.

As she mounted the steps, Adrienne looked at the two investigators over her shoulder.

"Yes. Isn't that permitted?" Her voice was strained.

Lissa walked past her and tore the yellow tape, letting it fall away.

"We're finished with it for now," she said, and stood aside. Adrienne walked past her and into the cabin. Uncomfortable in the presence of Lissa and Stanley, Adrienne simply looked around the room, stared for a few moments at the fireplace, then walked to the foot of the stairway and looked up.

"We always slept in the room on the right." A pause, and then she turned to the officers. "Could I be alone for a few minutes?"

"Yes, of course," King said.

Outside, Stan said, "If you want to keep looking around in the workshop, I'll just wait here." Lissa smiled and went down the steps. Morris stood close to the peeled porch rails and studied the reflections coming off the water in the river.

Back in the workshop, Lissa opened every drawer and cabinet. Too neat? Stan might be right, she mused. And realized that for the first time she had thought of him as Stan, not Lieutenant. And smiled. Her thoughts quickly refocused on the shop. Was everything too neat? Had Don Jackson really lived his training 24 hours a day? But wouldn't someone else realize that order was important. Wouldn't they have been careful to restore everything before leaving?

On her knees, the young woman used her flashlight to look under the workbench. About eight inches in from the front, hidden by a low shelf, she spotted what turned out to be a wooden spool wound with black silk fishing line. The label indicated that it was "15# test." She didn't know if that fifteen referred to pounds or a number, only that it was a very strong line.

Standing, she looked on the shelf where the rolls of line were kept. As she stared at them, she began to see a pattern, like soldiers lined up on parade, except along the very back row. A slight misalignment stood out. Nothing in the shop was dusty, so it would be impossible to say how long the roll on the floor had been there, or missing from the shelf. *But if Don had dropped it would he have left it? Say the fish were biting and he was in a big hurry to get out, planning to come back later. Still, that would have been weeks ago. His last visit hadn't seemed to be about fishing. What about Adrienne's? When had she last been here?*

ROANOKE, VIRGINIA

THE AUTOPSY ROOM in the state medical examiner's office was an unexceptional place, except perhaps for the temperature. Regardless of the season, the thermostat kept the room slightly on the cool side. Otherwise it was bright, the walls painted the green that seemed universal in older medical facilities, the equipment polished stainless steel or hard white porcelain. In the center of the room under an adjustable overhead lamp was a stainless steel table. It sat, canted slightly so that the head was lower than the foot. A microphone hung from the ceiling, placed to catch everything Dr. Mason or one of his colleagues would say as the autopsy proceeded.

Mason was at the table now, with his chief technician and a second pathologist. Don Jackson's body lay flaccid and exposed to the lights. Dr. Mason picked up a scalpel and made the first incision, a long, straight cut down the midline of the thorax.

Behind a barrier, with a large plate glass window, Stan Morris and Grady stood.

"Doubt there will be any surprises," the Lieutenant said, watching the process with interest.

"Not at this point, probably," Grady agreed.

"Any feeling for this case?" Morris turned briefly to the other man, then back to the view through the window.

"Yes," Grady replied. "But I always think the worst case scenario anyway. What has King said?"

Morris laughed. "She's closer with information than you are, Grady. It's like being with somebody in a museum, interested but not excited by what she sees."

"Damned good investigator. Learned that from me."

"What, not reacting?"

35

"That, and keeping it close until she knows what the story is."

The two turned back to the window. Mason and his colleague were examining the head. The technician, a strong looking younger man, was holding a bone saw, waiting for the order to cut. Mason and Theresa Morris, the other pathologist, were cautiously probing the wound on the side of the head.

"Dr. Morris related to you?" Grady said.

"Used to be."

"Oh."

"Conflict of interest." Stan smiled. "Been resolved about five years, now."

"Good."

"What about King?"

"What about her?"

"Anything but work on her mind?"

"We're in a tough business, Lieutenant. But you know that."

On the other side of the glass, the two doctors finished probing the head wound and were engaged in conversation. Mason looked at the two men behind the glass, then with Dr. Morris following, he left the table and walked to the opening in the partition. Behind them the technician was using the saw to open the skull.

"You found something." Grady's statement was flat, not a question.

"Something," Mason said. The four stood in a small circle, Theresa next to Mason, but decidedly closer to Grady than to Stanley. Mason opened his hand to reveal two dissimilar pellets; one larger than the other.

"We think these came from different size loads," Theresa offered.

"Of course, he could have discharged two shells when he fell," said Mason.

"You don't think so." Grady's voice remained un-emphatic.

"No." Theresa took up the thread. "It is possible that he was shot accidentally by his own gun, then finished with a second shot."

Stan finished the thought, "Or the other way around; shot first by someone laying for him, and then a second shot from his own gun to make it look like an accident."

Theresa said no more.

Grady picked the two pieces of metal out of Mason's hand. As he did so, a cell phone began ringing. All four went for their pockets like gun fighters on a dusty street. It was the Lieutenant's that was ringing.

"Morris." Pause. "Good work, Bert. Can we get a line on where to find 'em?" Another pause. The others continued examining the metal Grady now held. "Ok, Bert. As soon as you do. Thanks." The phone snapped shut. "The sheriff thinks they ID'd the men who reported the shooting. He's going to get me some addresses."

"Where are they?" Grady wanted to know.

"Pennsylvania. They come every year and set up camp above Jackson's place, but usually come into the woods from the road Jackson is on. The storekeeper came up with the ID from the hunting licenses he had written the day before. He was getting ready to send the records to Richmond and realized who they were."

"Be interesting to know what guns they were carrying that morning." Mason was still focused on the shot he and Theresa had found.

Grady took his own phone from an inside pocket. Turning away from the others, he walked out the door into the hallway. When Stan followed him a minute or two later, he was just putting the phone away.

"I'm going to send King up to Pennsylvania to interview these guys as soon as we know where they are."

"I'd like to go along, in case we need to bring them back. I can get a warrant ahead of time. They did leave the scene of a crime, if nothing else."

"Okay with me," Grady said. "Work it out with King."

LANCASTER, PENNSYLVANIA

LISSA KING AND STANLEY MORRIS arrived at the airport near Lancaster within an hour of each other. Lissa had used the short flight to consider how to connect the two hunters to Jackson's death, but saw no believable link. Stanley, arriving first, had waited for Lissa to rent the car that would take them the rest of the way. "Letting your office pay for it," he explained to Lissa.

"All the way," she agreed with a smile.

Once in the car, Stanley consulted the local area map, and Lissa followed his directions. It was after six when the pair arrived at the home of the older man, Art Wallace. His hunting partner, Eddie Kolwitz, joined them just as the interview was beginning.

"Is there a second room we could use?" Lissa asked Mr. Wallace. "It would save time if we interviewed you separately."

Wallace offered the use of the downstairs recreation room, and Stanley took Kolwitz to that room.

"Now, Mr. Wallace, can we get to the day you called 9-1-1?"

"Sure. What do you want to know?" The man was uncomfortable being interviewed, even though he was sure he wasn't in any trouble. "Got nothing to hide, I guess." He gave a little laugh.

"That's fine. Now first of all, how long had you been in Virginia on this trip? I understand you and Mr. Kolwitz hunt there frequently?"

"We'd come down the night before; got there about dark, and set up camp up near the top of Shenandoah. You know that place where you can park up there?"

King nodded. She had looked around the parking lot in front of the restored Confederate breastworks that spread across the mountain top.

"Usually we camp near the top, and then when we go out we drive down to the road where that cabin is. There's a public access trail about a mile down."

"Is that where you parked that morning?"

"Yeah. It takes about fifteen minutes to walk the trail to the National Forest where we can hunt. You know the trail?"

"I've walked part of it. Just to see where it crosses Mr. Jackson's land."

"Well, that part is the last part before you get to the forest itself. Eddie and I walked in, I'd guess about four in the morning. It isn't light at that hour, so we needed to use flashlights, but if you want to be in place when the birds get up, you need to do it before first light. Then you can settle down, you know? Get it all quiet again."

King looked at the man but said nothing. He was doing fine on his own, she thought.

"We settled in, I guess about twenty after four, still dark, still cold, but we have our favorite places all picked out ahead of time."

Lissa continued to look encouragingly at the man. He was beginning to look less confident, a little uncomfortable, perhaps. That was good.

"Anyway, we weren't the only ones in the woods that morning."

"Oh?"

"Not long after we were settled in, about four-thirty, we heard a shot down below us, I think."

"One shot?" The woman's voice was flat and disinterested.

"Well, maybe two. We weren't paying too much attention, except that it flushed some birds, and we were putting all our attention in that direction."

"Go on."

"Well, we got off a few shots, and Eddie got a fine gobbler, but I missed mine." Wallace laughed. "Luck of the hunt, I guess."

Lissa delayed questioning him further about how many shots he heard, letting him tell the story at his own pace.

"Anyway, about two, three hours later, must have been about eight o'clock, Eddie says, 'Let's go. I think it's over for the morning.' and I agreed. Wouldn't be much happening until near twilight, and we could use some breakfast. So we packed up and headed back."

"Were you planning to come back there in the afternoon?"

"No, we usually move to another campsite every night, going over to the next mountain the second night, then maybe on west the next night, and so on." The man stretched and looked out the window. "Night comes fast in those mountains. Not like here where it's flat." He stopped, his eyes seeing beyond his own suburban yard.

"Go on, Mr. Wallace."

"Yeah. Well, like I say, we decided to walk out. Now if no one is around, sometimes we'll head straight across the river, and that takes us across that fella's property."

"Mr. Jackson's?"

"Yeah. That's it. Saves some time, and when we get to the river, if it's up, we can cross his bridge. Dry feet are a good thing when you're in the woods." His face clouded slightly. He was crossing the Riversee land again. A smart man, he knew the woman wouldn't prompt him, and for a minute he just stopped talking.

Lissa checked her tape recorder, making sure there was

enough tape for the interview to continue uninterrupted.

"I guess it was about eight-fifteen when we came around the turn in the trail and stepped onto his land. We weren't rushing, so it may have been ten minutes before we came on him."

King gave what she hoped was an encouraging smile, but said nothing.

In the basement recreation room, Lieutenant Morris was at about the same point in his interview with Eddie Kolwitz. Eddie, younger and less phlegmatic, stayed with the story, but added more emotional words to his rendition. Words like "horrible" and "My god, look at that!" He was less introspective and still uncomfortable with what he and Wallace had discovered.

Morris, though not a hunter, knew enough of the sport to encourage Eddie with knowledgeable questions about the turkeys and about the condition of the woods.

"And then Jake, he goes, 'We'd better get back on the trail, Eddie,' and I go, 'right now, Jake,' and he says, 'Let's go.' So we headed back the way we came, until we got to the trail."

As King found with Wallace, the man was almost as concerned with trespassing as he had been with finding the body. He repeated again that, had they known Jackson would be at his cabin, they would never had diverted from the access trail. Morris just let the man explain himself again, before redirecting him to the events of that day.

"Tell me what you did when you got back to your truck."

"I put my bird in the cooler, then got in the passenger's side. Jake had already started the truck, and we just turned around and hauled - - just drove out to the highway."

In the end, both hunters told the same story, gave the same details, and ended with the same questioning look at their interrogators. It was seven o'clock when King and Morris left the house. Aside from their taped interviews, the investigators carried shotguns the two men owned, so that they could be examined for any possible connection with the death.

"We'll return these as soon as the FBI has had a chance to examine them," King said, handing each man a receipt for his guns.

"If we find there is sufficient reason to take this to a grand jury," Morris continued, "you may be subpoenaed to come and testify; to repeat what you've just told us."

The men nodded, but were obviously not looking forward to that happening.

In the car, Morris looked at the weapons in their carrying cases and said, "Losing their guns for a while is little enough cost for running off after they reported finding Jackson. I guess we can write them off."

"NO FLIGHTS EXCEPT TO DC," Morris said when he came back to where King was waiting.

She had already cleared the two gun cases with airport security, and checked in at the airline desk.

"You're welcome to come with me. My car is at the airport, and I can offer you a guestroom for the night."

Morris looked at her appraisingly. "I could probably get a short haul flight from the airport."

"If not, my offer stands."

"You going to brief Grady tomorrow?"

"First thing. You're welcome to come in for that."

ALEXANDRIA, VIRGINIA

THE FLIGHT WAS SHORT, LESS THAN FORTY MINUTES. The conversation dwelt on the interviews. Comparing notes, the two agreed that there was little gain for the time spent.

While Lissa went to pick up her luggage, Stan checked the airlines serving Roanoke. He caught up with her at the luggage area.

"The next direct flight's not 'til the tomorrow afternoon. Guest room still available?"

"Just waiting for a tenant."

"Carry your bag, Ma'am?" Taking the gun cases from her, they headed for the car park.

"Have you been to Alexandria before, Stan?" They were leaving the parkway that fed from Reagan National Airport, turning onto US-1.

"A few times." He looked out the window. "The airport was still Washington National the last time I was here, though."

"A lot of other things have changed, too." Her voice was less commanding now, more relaxed.

"Yeah," he said softly. "Yeah." He looked at the bright lights along King Street. "Named after you?"

"What? Oh! The street. Funny man. I'm not that old, thank you." She looked at him out of the corner of her eye. He was gazing into a distance she could not see. *Let it alone,* she counseled herself. *He'll talk when he's ready.*

A few blocks off King Street, near the waterfront, Lissa pulled into a private garage, using a keypad above the windshield to raise the door. An overhead mirror at the far end reflected the car and the closing door.

"Use that to check your lipstick?" Morris said, nodding toward the image.

"And anyone else's who might step in after me," she responded. "Came as part of a security package."

"Nice idea." He got out of the car and reached for the gun cases.

A door led to the rest of the ground floor, occupied by a neat utility room, an exercise machine, and closets. A carpeted stair led to what Lissa referred to as the first floor.

"It's a small house, so only the kitchen and living room are on this floor. Bedrooms are upstairs." She indicated another stairway. "When I bought the place it was much more formal, but the rooms were so small. Since it's just me, I knocked out a few walls and now I have a four-room house!" She smiled as she surveyed the results. "Every time I come back to it, I remember how much I like it."

"Seems ok for one person," Stanley agreed. "I live in a big empty house, myself. So much space I can never find anything."

Lissa looked at the clock on the white kitchen wall. It was almost half-past ten.

"I hadn't realized it was so late. Didn't we miss a meal somewhere?" She walked into the kitchen.

"Unless you count the bag of peanuts on the plane, yes we did. Is there a place open this late where we can get something?"

"Well, there's a seafood place down a block and around the corner. I know they serve until mid-night."

Picking up his jacket and her coat, Stan held hers out.

"Can we walk? I feel like I've been sitting too much today."

Using the front door, they left the house, walked down the brick steps and turned right.

"It's just around the corner," Lissa nodded to the right. As they turned, Stanley saw the rough-cut wooden sign, "Captain's Table," a few doors along.

Inside, the room was divided into several levels. At one side small high-backed booths were grouped around a large fireplace. Always a little cooler by the waterfront, the gas logs were lit, taking away the riverside dampness.

Taking the booth closest to the fire, Stanley hung their coats on the hook fixed to the end. They were quiet as they sat looking at the fire. A waitress came to the table. "Something to drink?"

"Yes, I think so," Stanley said. "What would you like?"

"Beer, whatever dark you have on tap," Lissa replied.

"Same for me," Stanley said, "and a menu, please." He turned his attention back to Lissa. He saw a woman of maybe 35 (she was a little older), blonde, tall, graceful, attractive in the way a woman is when she is assured, certain of what she knows, confident about her ability to handle what she finds in life. Her face was neither round nor narrow, but symmetrical, he thought. Nice dark eyes, large, the kind that could look innocent in one light, penetrating in another. *A woman of interest,* he mused. *Could there be something more?*

Lissa held the menu in front of her, scanning it, but at the same time letting her gaze include Stan. His dark hair (was it brown or reddish?) close-cropped in the manner of most of the cops she knew, but no mustache. His face was strong, eyes green, skin well toned. A man of about forty-five, she guessed (correctly, as it turned out), in good physical condition, no paunch, no flabbiness, strong. A quick mind, she had already discovered. Relaxed. A humorous turn from time-to-time. Civilized, was the word that came to mind.

"How did you find your way into the shadow world?" Stan wanted to know. "Were you recruited from college?"

"My father was with the agency."

"He's retired now?"

"He's dead, Stan."

"Oh. I'm sorry. Has it been long?"

"I was just out of college and not even with the agency then."

A silence, one of those that a good interrogator doesn't interrupt, kept the conversation alive. Stan looked at Lissa, watched as she closed her eyes, squeezed them tight, then held them that way for a second or two, as if she were seeing the re-run of a bad dream. Then, very quietly: "He didn't have to die." Again the silence. She looked at Stan, then away, out the window into the darkness. "It shouldn't have been him."

Stan wanted to ask questions, hoping that he could open up this tightly held, exciting woman. Instead he allowed her the time he felt she needed.

"It's why I applied to the agency." Another long pause. "I wanted to understand so many things."

"What kind of things?"

"Why he did that work in the first place. Why he held on, despite the danger, despite losing my mother, and for a long time, me."

Again Stan waited for her.

"You see, there was a long time after they divorced, when I was three, that I didn't know my father. I knew other kids had them, but I didn't. And my mom wasn't interested in replacing him, either. She loved him, I think, until the day she died."

"How old were you then?"

"I was in my first year of college. Mom was diagnosed with cancer and died about six months after the first examination."

"Awful."

"Unfair, is what I thought at the time."

"Your dad still out of your life at that point?"

"Yes. When she got the diagnosis, and the prognosis, Mom called him and told him. They had been in contact over the years, you see, but he had stayed away from me until then. I guess Mom impressed on him that I was facing being all alone, and that it was time he stepped up and did more for me than pay bills."

"Had he been good about that?"

"I think so. We never lacked for the things we needed, including my high school and college. We lived nicely, you know; not grand, but nice. A house in a decent neighborhood in Arlington, across from a small park. Mom worked for the Navy in one of the buildings nearby, and I went to good schools, had friends, did growing-up things just like everybody else. And of course, I wasn't the only one with an absent father. I always thought I was okay about it, because so many of my friends had divorced parents, and some of them seemed to always be changing step-fathers. At least we were contained and close, my mom and I."

"How was it when your dad came into your life? Had you ever seen him up to that point?"

"He came to my high school graduation. That was the first time I had seen him since I was three. I was resentful and probably a little cold to him that day. It took a while for me to understand why he had stayed away, and could still love me."

"You think he did?"

"Stan, I know he did. It took time, but after Mom died, and I began to spend time with him during school vacations, I realized that he thought he was protecting me by not letting me get close to him, knowing he would be here one day, then suddenly disappear, maybe for a long time, then pop up again as if he'd never been away. That was the root of the trouble in the first place. Mom couldn't live with not knowing where he was, or I guess, *if* he was. That can be hard on a woman."

"I know about that, Lissa. Theresa went through the same thing with me in the early years, and then, in a way, we sort of did it to each other. It isn't a very stabilizing way to live."

"No. I think I might have gotten used to it a little more easily than Mom, since I wasn't ever expecting him to be there. When he was it was fine, when he wasn't, well that was more what I was used to anyway."

"Do you miss him, still?"

"More than I ever thought I would. More than I would like, too." She looked into the firelight. "But I think I'm finally coming to terms with it."

When they had eaten, and added another beer to the tab, it was nearly midnight. Stan picked up the check as Lissa reached into her purse for her wallet.

"My treat," Stan said, handing the waitress enough to cover the check and her tip. "Haven't enjoyed a seafood dinner in a long time. In fact," he smiled, "haven't enjoyed dinner in a long time, period!"

As they walked the block-and-a-half back to the house, Stan took her arm, and it felt right to Lissa.

In the living room, the telephone answering machine was blinking. Pushing the button, Lissa heard Grady's voice: "I'll be expecting you at 0730 in the morning, King. If Morris can hang around, bring him along. Goodnight."

Lissa and Stan looked at each other and laughed.

"No secrets in our work," she said.

THE EARLY MORNING SUN SLIPPED BETWEEN THE SLATS of the Venetian blinds and fell on Lissa. She lay comfortably on her side, her head propped on her hand, and she was looking between the slats at the gold and red of the dawn light. The night before, at the top of the stair, Stan had taken her gently in his arms and kissed her. "Good night," he had said, and gone into his room. *That was exactly right*, Lissa thought. *It could have been very awkward. Later, maybe, but now there is work still to do.* And work had always been Lissa's answer to the conflict between reality and desire. It would have to be that way at least until she could be certain this man would understand her

NORTHERN VIRGINIA

"WHAT WE KNOW SO FAR," Lissa was saying, "is that there is reason to go beyond a simple accident." She and Lieutenant Morris were in Grady's office, around the small conference table in the middle of the room. A laptop on the table, connected to a small projector, flashed pictures on the screen as the agent reviewed what was known about Don Jackson's death. "Although the body, as we first found it, told a story that pointed to accidental death, it may have been just a little too perfect."

"Too perfect to be done by one person, or at least one person acting on the spur of the moment," Stan offered.

Grady and King looked at the Lieutenant.

"I know we have a slight indicator," he continued, nodding toward the two pieces of steel shot in a plastic bag on the table, "but unless ballistics can demonstrate beyond a doubt that these are not fragments from a single load, we aren't going to have a case."

"You mean as in 'court case'?" Grady rumbled. "Not our job."

"We'll let the state worry about that, Stan," Lissa added. "We need to know what happened, need to know if there was a security breach, need to look ahead if there was, and act on that."

"And if it was an accident?"

"If it was an accident, or if it wasn't a security issue, we aren't in your thoughts at all." Lissa looked at Stan as she finished speaking.

"Do I get to know what you don't find?"

"We aren't in it, Lieutenant," Grady concluded, "unless it touches us."

What touches you? Stan wondered, before saying, "Ok with me. What's next?"

FBI BUILDING, WASHINGTON, D.C.

NEXT WAS A DRIVE INTO THE CITY. Lissa had arranged to meet a contact at the J. Edgar Hoover building. The two guns from Pennsylvania would go to the ballistics experts. Flashing her pass, she was about to pull through into the building's garage when the security guard stopped her.

"I need to check your passenger, Ms. King." Lissa looked at Stan. He had anticipated the guard and was already handing his Virginia State Police ID across Lissa. The guard nodded, said "Ok," and waved them through.

"You been here before, Stan?"

"A few times." There was a hint of something unsaid in his answer.

Was there a hint of a smile in his voice? She hoped so. Mixing business with your personal life was always risky, she thought.

Taking the guns from the car, the pair headed for the elevator. Getting off on one of the upper floors, Lissa looked around.

"I think it's this way," Stan said, and turned right. Lissa

followed him through a door. The receptionist looked up. A flicker of recognition crossed her face, and she smiled at the two visitors.

"Agent Rasmussan is expecting us." Lissa felt, more than saw, the man at her side stiffen, but didn't process the information. At that moment a heavy-set, olive complected man came into the reception area.

"Hello, King," he began, then stopped and looked at Stan. "Morris! Well its been a long time."

"So it has. So it has."

"Thought you had gone to the state. Didn't know you were back with the feds."

"Not, Raz. Still with the state, but King and I are working on a case together."

"Well come on back. I think I'm not the only guy in the shop who'll remember you." Turning, he led the way.

Lissa held back for a moment, looking at her companion, now moving with Rasmussan through the door. In the large room where the agents in Raz's section worked, they turned over the guns and King filled out the request for ballistics comparison. She also included the small fragments recovered by the medical examiners. While she was busy, Rasmussan and Morris and two other agents gathered around another desk. From the tone of the voices, and the occasional laughter, King knew the men were catching up on each other's lives. Shaking her head, she frowned, then smiled. *Exactly who is this man*, she wondered, *and what does it mean for me? Certainly more to him than I had thought. A bit more complex, maybe even . . . dangerous.*

IN THE CAR AGAIN, headed for the airport, both were silent. Finally, as they pulled up to the passenger unloading area, Lissa looked at Stan for a long moment.

"I'm still getting used to the FBI thing. You certainly don't share information, do you?"

"Lissa, that was a long time ago. For a lot of reasons. I'd like to tell you about it, about the reasons, but not now."

"When? Next time we work on a case together?" Her voice was only a little shrill, she realized. "I mean, I guess I really don't have a 'need to know,' but, well, Stan, I'd like to know what we're -- I'm getting into. If I'm getting into anything." *Shut up*, she told herself, *this has nothing to do with Don Jackson.*

"Are you going back to the scene?"

"Maybe, but I don't think so. I think I have done what I need to do there."

"Can I see you in a couple of days? Maybe have dinner?" He looked at his watch. "I have about five minutes to get to the ticket counter, Lissa. I'll call you later." He closed the door, stepped back, and waited for her to drive away. She waited for him to turn and head for the door. Then they both moved at once: he to the car, she to the window. Sticking his head in, he gave her a gentle, promising kiss, and then was gone. A security guard waved her impatiently into the traffic lane.

An hour later, back in her office, she was thinking about her interview with Adrienne. Grady came in without knocking, and stood in front of her desk. "You and the trooper seemed to get along pretty well."

"He's a senior investigator, Grady, not a trooper. And he's been very helpful."

"I know." There was almost a smile in the man's voice. Almost, but not quite. "Probably good at speaking 'country.'"

"He used to be FBI."

"I knew that, King. And a good one from what I hear. Now let's talk some more about what you think of this case." Taking the chair opposite Lissa, Grady prepared to listen. He knew his chief assistant would have a well-developed working hypothesis by now.

Lissa sat back, resting her elbows on the arms of her chair, and looked above and past Grady.

"Three things. One, it was not an accident. Two, his wife is involved. Three, if she did it, could it have been something other than a crime of passion." The expression on her face said, *Where did that come from? I haven't even given a thought to that idea.*

Grady's face registered nothing.

"I mean," Lissa continued, "something or someone else is involved. Someone we haven't picked up on yet."

"You said you talked to her the day after the murder. What did you get from that?"

"It wasn't just what I got from her. It was the whole scene, the house and shop buildings, the feel of the place, and yes, her reaction to finding us still in charge of the place."

"Tell me about the place."

"Neat. Orderly. Everything clean and in its place." Her mind retrieved the pictures of the buildings and the yard she had stored. "Except a roll of fishing line. Black silk, very fine, very strong." She paused and saw again the wooden spool with the line on it. "That had ended up under a workbench. A workbench that had no dust or debris of any kind under it. Just like the rest of the place."

Grady nodded but said nothing.

"You sensed something like that, didn't you?"

"Let's just say I'm suspicious when grief is cold."

"What really makes me suspicious," Lissa said, measuring her words, "what makes me suspicious is that in a place like that county, nobody noticed a stranger."

"What stranger?"

"That's just the point. If you wanted to hide, a place like that would cover you before the door closed. But if someone came looking for you, even without asking, they would be observed, noted, remarked on. Nobody seems to have seen anyone they didn't know."

"Go have another talk with the widow."

WASHINGTON, D.C.

ADRIENNE WAS SITTING UP, the pillows bunched behind her, the covers tucked primly under her chin. Jason lay on his side, his back to her. Breathing slowly and quietly.

"Are you awake?"

The man moved as if in sleep, then murmured, "Uh huh. Yes" His voice was sleepy sounding.

"I'm not sure that coming here was a good idea."

"Just consoling the widow."

"Not funny."

"Didn't mean it to be." He turned over and looked at her. "What difference could it make? Really?" He sat up and tried to take her in his arms.

"Not now. I want to talk."

"About?"

"What we do."

"Which part?"

"This part, Jason. Making love, being together. It's so dangerous."

"Perhaps that's what you like about it."

"No, no I don't. I hate sneaking around, being afraid of discovery. Oh, Jason, if we were found out you would lose your assistantship, I couldn't mentor you, I'd probably lose my professorship -- it would be dreadful." Adrienne began to cry.

"I tell you, professor, you have nothing to worry about."

Muted by the distance from the bedroom to the front door, the chime broke into their conversation.

"Oh, god! Someone at the door."

"Want me to go?" Jason's voice was just a little cold.

"Jason! No! Maybe whoever it is will go away."

The musical sound repeated. Adrienne threw back the covers and sat on the edge of the bed, her back to Jason. He reached for her, but she shrugged him away, stood, and picking up her robe from the floor, slipped into it as she left the room. The door closed softly behind her.

"Hello, Mrs. Jackson. I hope I didn't wake you." Lissa glanced at her watch. Only nine-thirty.

"I -- I'm a little slow getting out this morning."

"I hope this isn't an inconvenient time," the agent said, stepping through the door held open for her. "I just wanted to return some things to you." In her hands were two thick brown envelopes. A laptop in a case was slung from her shoulder.

"Was any of it helpful?" Adrienne was a little vague about what had been taken during a quick search the day of Don's death. She tried to sound disinterested.

"More of a routine check to make sure nothing in Mr. Jackson's possession would be compromising to the agency." Lissa sensed that the widow reacted to the word "compromise." Putting the envelopes on the hall table, Lissa nodded toward the door to the library.

"Would you like me to put these things back for you?"

"Yes. Fine."

As Lissa stepped into the library she heard another door open, and was aware that Adrienne was holding a hurried and somewhat breathless conversation with someone else. She turned just in time to see a man walk past the door. Then she heard him leave the apartment.

"That was my teaching assistant. He came by to pick up some notes for this morning's lecture."

It was so obvious to King that the woman was lying that

she didn't even bother to challenge her. It was obvious that Adrienne was aware of the lameness of the explanation.

"Could we talk?" Lissa stood aside to let the other woman enter the room.

"What about?" Adrienne's eyes showed a momentary panic.

"Mrs. Jackson, did your husband usually go to the cabin alone?"

Adrienne tried to focus on what had prompted the questions, but couldn't find a reason.

"Lately, yes."

"Lately being when?"

"The last few years. The last three or four. He seemed to need the time alone more than he had in the early years." Adrienne knew she shouldn't embellish her answers, but couldn't help herself.

"We always went together at first. When we were dating, and then when we were married." The woman looked out the window, as if she were seeing the place a hundred and fifty miles away. She said no more.

Lissa waited. When nothing more came from Adrienne, she started another question: "How often did he go, in say the last six months?"

"It seems like it was every time he had more than a day off. He loved that place so. He'd had it for years before we met, you know. I think he always felt uncomfortable in this apartment."

"This was yours before you met, wasn't it?"

On safer ground, now, the woman relaxed. "Yes. I had

given up thinking about marriage I guess, and buying this apartment seemed a way to commit my life to what it was. That was almost ten years before I met Don."

"Didn't you like being at the cabin? It's pretty isolated down there."

"Oh, there are plenty of people; fine people, the ones I met. Mostly farmers and loggers, and a few shopkeepers. A lot of people from this area, too. They have weekend places and retirement homes, and sometimes we would get together. Mostly the men knew each other from hunting down there over the years. It was a wonderful place to relax, and just be together. Yes, it was," she reassured herself. "Don taught me to fish, and I even liked hunting." her voice faded away. Her thoughts seemed to collide, and suddenly her eyes were wet. She shook her head.

"I'm sorry. I was thinking about how it was before --," her voice trailed off.

"Before what?" Lissa's question was delivered softly, as if she felt the anguish Adrienne had suddenly exposed.

Adrienne moved to one of the chairs beside the cold fireplace. As she sat, her robe opened briefly, exposing her naked body underneath.

Picking up lecture notes, my foot!

Adrienne looked up at Lissa. Her face was wistful. She looked again at the fireplace.

"Before all of this. When we were still discovering each other." She shook her head. "Do you know what that is like?"

The touch of Stan's hand on her arm flashed into Lissa's mind. "I think so."

"Then you know the way a man can seem to change. But they are really just revealing themselves a little at a time." She paused, then went on: "A woman does too, of course. Change, I mean. But I think more dramatically. Perhaps none of us are the people we seem to be."

AS SHE REACHED HER CAR, the cell phone in Lissa's pocket vibrated. Pulling it out as she opened the door, she saw Stan's number on the display. She put the phone in the holder on the console, closed the door and started the engine. Checking the traffic, she pulled out and headed back to her office. Just who the graduate assistant was, his relationship to the widow, while obvious on the surface, might not be what it seemed; might have more importance than simply consoling this woman who held her emotions close.

NORTHERN VIRGINIA

THE PHONE RANG AGAIN as the agent slipped into her parking place at the agency. Again it was Lieutenant Morris. This time she flipped the cover and answered.

"Hello, Stan."

"I have something that might be important," he began without preamble. "Something that showed up in a traffic stop about an hour after Jackson was shot."

"Do you think it's significant?"

"Could be. Want me to read it to you?"

"Can you send it? I'll be in the office in about two minutes."

"Sure. It's on its way. And Lissa - - "

"Yes?"

"Call me. I really want to see you."

The fax machine was still printing when Lissa reached her desk. Putting her coat on the hook behind the door, she walked to the machine and began reading the first page. It was a report from a trooper assigned to the interstate serving the Shenandoah Valley. Lissa picked up the internal telephone.

"Grady, I've got something coming in from Morris. Are you free?"

"I'll be right there."

As Grady walked into the office Lissa handed him the first sheet. She had the second page in her hand, reading it.

"What's this?"

"It's a report that came up from a routine traffic stop on I-81. According to the report, there was an accident involving a vehicle that left the scene. It happened about an hour after we think Jackson was shot."

"So how does that tie in with the traffic stop?"

"Well, it doesn't, exactly. But Stan, Lieutenant Morris, thought there might be a connection." She handed the second page to Grady.

"I see. Two men with diplomatic plates and passports traveling north. Romania." Grady was silent for a moment, then said, "Could be."

"Do we know these names?"

"This one." Grady pointed to the first name on the list. "Constantinescu. I believe there's a connection to Jackson."

"Not from this last trip, though?"

"From something that went down years ago."

"I'll talk to the embassy. I have a contact there."

Grady left the room as Lissa picked up the phone and at the same time, fished a small address book from the middle drawer of her desk. The number she dialed connected almost instantly. The voice of the woman who answered was lightly accented.

"Lissa here. How are you?"

"Fine, Lissa. We have not spoken in some time."

"I have a favor to ask."

"I will try."

"Two men," Lissa hardly hesitated over the two names. "Georghe Constantinescu and Ilie Lazarovici. Are they available for me to talk to?"

There was a long pause.

"Marika? Is this a bad call?"

"No. Ok to call. Only, names not good."

"Not with the embassy?"

"Gone home. Back to Romania."

"But they were here?"

"Just for few days. Then go home."

"Are these 'ok' people, Marika?"

"Yes. Ok. Trade mission. Friends. Ok." The connection was broken.

As Lissa put the receiver back in the cradle, her cell phone chimed. It was Stan.

"Good timing. I just got off the other phone with the embassy."

"Any happiness there?"

"No. Both men have left the country. Too bad your reporting system wasn't faster."

Stan added a comical drawl for effect. "We do things a little more slowly down here in the country, Ma'am." He paused: "But we do follow up. I think you can let them go."

"Why?"

"We went back to the people they reported meeting in Blacksburg. Some technical developers at Tech."

"My contact said they were trade mission types."

"Right. They were at the university for a few days, and checked out of their motel very early the morning they were interviewed. The timing would eliminate a stop anywhere but where our people talked to them."

But why was the embassy so tense about them? Lissa held the thought and instead, said: "Well, thanks Stan. It may save us from an unproductive inquiry. Another one."

"Lissa?"

She didn't answer.

"You still there?"

"Yes."

"I can be in Alexandria in a few hours."

"I know."

"Your house?"

"I'll be home by seven."

ALEXANDRIA, VIRGINIA

IT WAS CLOSER TO SIX-THIRTY when Lissa arrived home. In the kitchen she put a steak and some fresh vegetables in the refrigerator. She moved more of the dark beer from the pantry into the refrigerator, too. Then she went upstairs. *I'm primping,* she thought to herself. *He just wants to talk, and I'm worried about how I look. Smart girl. I've deduced that I'm as interested in him as he seems to be in me! Why now? Why has it taken me so long to find someone?*

It was a few minutes after seven when the doorbell chimed. From the top floor landing, Lissa looked out the window and saw Stan. He was looking uncomfortable, exposed, holding a bunch of flowers. He looked up just as she left the window and hurried down the stairs.

DINNER WAS OVER AND THEY WERE STANDING ON THE SMALL BALCONY overlooking the equally small courtyard behind the house. The night was mild, the smell of autumn in the air. Looking between the buildings around them they saw the waterfront, and watched a sailboat heading out on a moonlight cruise.

"When I lived up here the waterfront wasn't a very attractive place."

"When you were with the Bureau?"

"Yes. We lived across the river, in what was called the New Southwest. Modern condos built over what had been pretty poor neighborhoods. Back when urban renewal was the big movement in DC. By the time we got there it was just another neighborhood. Nice, but not the up-scale inner-city it was supposed to be."

Lissa, like the good interviewer she was, let him go on for a while longer, knowing that whatever he had to say would eventually find its way out. For now, she understood that he was trying to find a comfortable place to begin. What? A confession? A personal history? She encouraged him by not interrupting. When he paused and didn't seem ready to go on, she looked at the city across the water and asked: "Did you like working at the Bureau?"

"It was good work, Lissa. Challenging. It was what I had wanted to do since I was a kid."

They were standing close together now, their hands on the balcony railing. She put her hand on his. "Why did you give it up, Stan?" She was looking up at him, her eyes asking more questions than her words.

He looked down at her face, then without answering, he bent his head and kissed her, gently, on the lips. She responded almost immediately, and for a while there were no words.

"I didn't mean to do that." His voice was a hoarse whisper.

"I did," Lissa heard herself saying. Her voice was equally subdued. Then she added: "But I really do want to know."

"Why I left." It was a statement, almost like a title for a

report. "This is really hard, Lissa, because I still think it makes me sound weak. And I'm not really good in that role."

She encouraged him by taking his hand and bringing it to her cheek. Looking up into his eyes, she saw that he was smiling.

"It isn't something terrible," he went on. "I'm not the first to give up something 'for the woman I love' -- loved." His open hand stroked her cheek. "Theresa felt I was neglecting her, spending too much time with my work, traveling too often on assignments I couldn't control. So after trying to satisfy both my job and my wife, I decided she had to come first. And for a while it seemed to work. We were spending more time together, we were happier, and in fact, the State Police work is in a lot of ways more satisfying, probably because most investigations are concluded faster, and we go to court sooner. Not always, but a lot of the time."

"Then what happened?"

"Terry's a pathologist. A very good one, by the way. She was working for a big hospital corporation, and sometimes I would talk to her about crime scene stuff. Questions I had. Things like that. The irony is that after all of her complaints about working odd schedules and distant places, she applied to the state medical examiner's office. She was attracted to the crime-solving part of it. And suddenly we had no life again. It sounds trite, I guess, but soon she had no time for us, and at the same time, we were too often on opposite ends of a case. That led to conflicts we never got around." There was a long pause.

Does it have to be that way, Lissa wondered?

Stan finished his story: "But that was a long time ago, Lissa. There was simply an incompatibility that no amount of job changing or work scheduling would ever fix. For two smart people who specialize in analysis and deduction, it took us a hell of a long time to figure that out."

"You're still friends, aren't you?"

"Well, we don't see each other often enough to test that, but neither are we unable to be in each other's company. We just don't go out of our way to do it. Besides, she married again a few years ago. Another doc. I think they understand each other better."

The breeze off the river was still pleasant, so it was not the temperature of the air that sent them back inside.

WASHINGTON, D.C.

ADRIENNE WATCHED AS JASON WALKED TO THE CHAIR where his clothes were piled. For the first time, she realized, she was completely disinterested. He began to dress. His back to her, she let her eyes rest on his blonde hair. He still favored the long, European look that, even in its rumpled state, appeared planned and tidy.

"You're going? Just getting up and leaving? Is that it?" Her voice was, curiously, dispassionate.

"It's time to go, Adrienne."

"For now, or is this 'goodbye'?" Her voice was without emotion.

"You know the answer to that as well as I, Adrienne."

"I know it's time, Jason. Now get out and be out of my office by the time I get there." She turned away, pulled the covers up over her own nakedness, and closed her eyes. She didn't open them until she heard the outer door close.

There can be no going back this time. It is over. It should never have started, I know. Adrienne was standing in the shower, letting the water wash over her. She had turned the multi-jet spray from needle-sharp to gentle caress, and let the steaming, streaming flow take away a tiredness she had only just discovered. *How could I have let this happen? A student. Not even a colleague.* Was the disgust she felt because she had started an affair, or was it that the affair involved a student? She didn't know. She only knew that what had seemed a harmless dalliance had turned into something passionate on her part - more passionate than anything she had ever felt. *Oh, Don. I did love you. I thought I'd never find anyone to love for a lifetime.* Tears mixed with the water running over her face. *But where was the passion? How foolish to find I needed that too, and so late.*

Before her mirror, Adrienne studied her face, looking to see if what she felt, what she had become, was on her face, in her eyes. She could see nothing but her own familiar self: high cheekbones, long dark hair slightly graying, long neck still unlined., her body only lightly touched by middle-age. No, she saw nothing unfamiliar. Nor, she realized, could she feel anything. Don was gone, Jason had left her (or she had sent him away), and she had only herself. And who was that?

THE MORNING LIGHT CUT ACROSS THE UNIVERSITY QUADRANGLE and into Adrienne's office. The dawn had been chilly, and the sun was welcome. She sat with her back to the desk. Her eyes were focused far beyond the glass; the images she saw not those in front of her window. The door behind her opened.

"I think we need to talk," Jason began.

Without turning or even moving her head to see his pale reflection in the glass, she said in a listless voice: "I've been expecting you."

"I don't know what is happening between us, Adrienne, but I think it is not good." Jason was tense and it showed. His pronunciation became studied, over precise, characteristic of someone who has been schooled to remove all trace of a regional or foreign accent. Every word was fully shaped, every vowel sounded, every word separated like the words on a computer screen typed by an expert. "We must stop seeing each other, I think," he pronounced. "We can not be seen together."

"You are weakening, aren't you Jason?" Her voice was suddenly sad and tired.

"What is it that you are saying?"

"You know perfectly well what I'm saying."

"It is only to protect you that I say this."

"To protect your precious degree."

"Not so, professor. Not at all. That is not what this is about."

"Oh, isn't it? Isn't that what your love-making has been about all the time, Jason?" She turned to face him. "Do you think I'm that stupid? Did you ever think I could have been bored and lonely, instead of madly in love with you? Even a woman sometimes needs a plaything. Or is that too base a sentiment for you?"

Jason stared at the woman he thought he knew; thought he had all figured out. He stepped back. Saying nothing more, he turned and left the office. A few minutes passed before Adrienne heard the outer door close, and knew she was alone.

Alone with her thoughts, alone with her memories, alone with her unhappiness. *What do I have now? What have I let happen?*

What have we done?" She sank into the big executive chair and began to cry softly at first, then in great heaving sobs, as for the first time the real consequences of her actions revealed themselves to her.

ALEXANDRIA, VIRGINIA

THE SAME SUN BROACHED THE VENETIAN BLIND that covered the window in Lissa's bedroom. She lay on her side, her head propped on her hand, her face just touched by the morning light. A little, private smile added illumination. Her eyes were focused on the face beside her, relaxed, stubbled, and that face too was smiling. And then it spoke: "Coffee. Coffee would be nice." Lissa bent over and kissed Stan, and for a little while longer coffee went unmade.

"I'm not on call this weekend, Lissa. And the weather looks perfect for a day in the country. What do you say?"

"Does that mean we are going to have an informal relationship?"

"In a formal way."

She snuggled against him again.

WASHINGTON, D.C.

STAN'S CAR, AN ALL-BLACK EX-STATE POLICE CRUISER, was moving slowly across the university grounds. He wanted to look at the campus where Adrienne taught. He had not been there for several years, and he thought it would help him understand the people involved. The widow and the graduate student were "persons of interest" to the two investigators, and Lissa understood the need for a complete mental picture. "Geography" it was called in the classes she had attended; getting to know the people and the places where they played out their lives. It went beyond mere curiosity. By building as complete a picture as possible, it became easier to spot the cracks in the facade, or the holes in an otherwise solid story. Who were these people? What could their lives mean in Don Jackson's death? That was what this trip was all about.

From her office window Adrienne watched the car come around the circle and past her office window. She recognized the driver and passenger. The car stopped for a minute or two in front of the building. Adrienne passed her hand over her eyes, letting it block the picture she saw through the window, but it was less disturbing than the picture of Don she saw when she closed her eyes. When she moved her hand, the car was gone. *Why were they here? Why come to the campus on a Saturday morning just to drive by my office? That woman from Mr. Grady's office may be a little smarter than I thought, but what do they want?*

The car moved smoothly and quietly across the campus. Ahead of them, walking quickly along the sidewalk, they passed a casually-dressed man hurrying along with a large cardboard box in his arms. As they passed him they both turned their heads and looked at him.

"That's Jason Arno. Adrienne's graduate assistant and, I suspect, her lover. I wonder what he's doing with what looks like a box full of file folders?"

"Running away from home?

"I don't know that it was 'home,' but whatever it was, I don't think it is anymore. I felt a tension . . . had the impression they had a fight over something the other morning when I surprised them at her apartment."

"Guilty looks?"

"Killing looks was more like it."

"The professor having a little adventure, maybe?"

"Maybe a little too much adventure."

"No such thing as too much adventure." He placed his hand over hers.

"Damn! I forgot this was a day off," Lissa laughed. *A sweet laugh,* Stan thought.

Still in her office, Adrienne picked up the telephone. Her hand hesitated over the buttons, before she punched in the numbers for Jason's cell. The effort resulted only in the recorded message inviting her to leave her number. *Of course. He can see I'm calling.* Putting the receiver back in the cradle, she vowed to make no more calls to him. Instead, she picked up a campus directory, confirmed another number, and again picked up the phone. Dialing, she sat back and waited for the answer. After eight rings, yet another answering machine responded. This time she left a message: "Albert, Adrienne here. I need to discuss a change in my graduate assistant's status. I'll be at home after," she looked at her watch, "after eleven. Thanks." Hanging up the phone, she stood slowly, looked to make sure her computer was off and her desk locked. Picking up her purse, she left the office, locking the door behind her, and walked slowly to her car in the faculty lot. *Can I go to Riversee?* She wondered. *Will I ever be able to go there again? Maybe that is where I should be.* With that thought in her mind, Adrienne drove to her Pennsylvania Avenue home.

NORTHERN VIRGINIA

"THE TWO MEN FROM ROMANIA," Grady began, "were on our payroll ten years ago." Lissa was sitting across from Grady in his office. "I just turned that up in a conversation with Sam Hamilton. He's trying to find out from their handler if either one of them knew Don."

"How long will that take?"

"The handler retired two or three years ago. He lives in the same county where Jackson's cabin is, but he doesn't seem to be at home."

"Anything to the fact that he lives there, do you think?"

"Probably not. Although there are several people from here who live in that part of the world."

"A good place to hide, maybe," Lissa said.

The phone on Grady's desk buzzed. "Lieutenant Morris on line three," said the voice on the intercom.

"Lieutenant," Grady growled.

"Something new to think about, Mr. Grady."

"Go ahead."

"I had a conversation with the sheriff, Bertrand, this morning."

"Well?

"He called me to say that he'd been talking to the storekeeper in Whitechapel."

Grady switched the call to the speaker phone. Morris's voice reached out to Grady and King.

"Jacob told Bertrand that Mrs. Jackson was also a hunter. Had her own rifle and a shotgun. Used to buy her ammo at his store."

"Bought any recently?"

"Not since last season. Anyway, we didn't turn up any guns made for a woman when we went through the cabin. Agent King and your people, that is."

"Yes, I am aware of that."

"The storekeeper also says he heard a car the morning of the shooting."

"I imagine he hears lots of cars go by."

"Well, yes, but for someone like that, when he 'hears a car,' it's because it isn't one he hears every day."

Lissa leaned toward the desk, to be nearer the speaker phone. "Lieutenant?"

"Hello, King. I thought you might be in on this. What is it?"

"What was different that it made him remember it?"

"He said that he heard a car about five o'clock. Usually there is some traffic about four-thirty, and again about five-thirty, give or take a few minutes, so this was one that he registered as being at the wrong time."

"What took him so long to remember it?"

"Well, he says that he had a feeling there was something he

should tell us, but it only came to him this morning."

"Anything else?" King asked.

"Bert says the car could have just been someone late for work, but he doesn't think so."

"How does that fit with the timeline?"

"The hunters put the shot at four-forty five. That would work with someone leaving pretty quickly after that."

"Where was the car coming from?"

"Storekeeper says he couldn't tell from his house. It might have come from the gravel road or down the mountain on the main highway. His house is east of the store, and set back a bit. Bert says that would block any pinpointing of the location."

"Thanks, Morris," Grady said. "We'll factor that in and see where it takes us."

"Ok. But it might be worth another trip to the cabin to see if your guys missed something."

"I'll suggest it to agent King," Grady said dryly. "There seem to be a lot of little things to sort out now. Before anybody does any more looking, I think we need to lay all of this out together."

"Sounds like a plan," Morris replied. "Your place?"

Grady looked at Lissa. "Tomorrow at ten too early?"

"I'll be there. Want to bring the sheriff in on this? I can meet him and bring him with me."

Lissa's eyes turned abruptly away from Grady.

"Yes. As long as we're digging in his yard he might as well join us. He seems to pick up things pretty quickly."

"Tomorrow at ten, then." The phone clicked off.

GRADY AND KING WERE ALREADY IN THE CONFERENCE ROOM when Morris and Bertrand arrived. As the two visitors fixed coffee for themselves, Stan and Lissa looked at each other and then the four moved to the conference table.

"I'll ask Agent King to begin the review," Grady said, "since this is her case. But before I do, let me set the ground rules. First, we have no conclusions at this time, only questions. This morning is for us to put all the questions on the table and get them in some kind of order. Second, some of what we will have to share with you is classified information. I know I don't have to explain that to either of you. And third, we need to decide what is the most likely lead, and pursue it quickly. Too much time is going by and we have no answers. King?"

Lissa stood up and walked to the white board at the end of the room. With a marker she wrote:

Don Jackson - Died October 24

Cause of death - gunshot wound to head

Primary evidence - possible accidental shooting by Jackson

Medical examiner - significant evidence of two separate and different guns involved

Only one found at scene

"I put these simple statements up so that we are all starting from the same place. We are discarding the 'possible self-inflicted' explanation, and assuming that if -- and I emphasize 'if' -- if there was an accident, there was someone else involved. The question is who that person might be."

"I'm not familiar with the 'two gun' theory," Sheriff Bertrand interjected. "What's that about?"

"Mr. Grady and Lieutenant Morris were both at the medical examiner's office, Sheriff."

Morris turned to Bertrand. "The M. E. found two sizes of pellets in the brain. His associate, who has done a lot of ballistics research, verified that no known shell would combine those two pellet sizes. Something I just heard last night before I left my office is that the FBI lab has analyzed the powder residue and found two different kinds."

"We haven't had the FBI report yet," Lissa said, her voice reflecting her surprise.

"No. It was something I asked the medical examiner's office to get for me. I had the information by phone. The written report will come later today."

Lissa absorbed the "something I asked the medical examiner's office to get for me," and returned to the white board.

"There is also this," and she wrote on the board:

Hunters in area at time of shooting - cleared

Foreign operators in area - possible connection

"Thanks to your office, sheriff, we were able to locate the two men who found Jackson, and made the 9-1-1 call. Lieutenant

Morris and I were able to rule out these men as likely suspects. One FBI report we do have," her voice only a little sarcastic, "indicates that neither of their shotguns were involved in the shooting."

"Did you really think it was a possibility?" Bertrand asked.

"Only if it were an accident," Morris said. "One of them might have been the gun."

"Could be they both shot at the same bird," Bertrand drawled. The idea hung there for a moment before Grady took it away:

"Wrong size pellets in their shells."

"Our interviews convinced us neither man was in any way involved," Lissa added. "We, Lieutenant Morris and I, interviewed them separately and came to the same conclusion."

"As for the foreign operators," Stan nodded toward the whiteboard, "they were interviewed in connection with an accident on the interstate early that morning, but they had left the country by the time the report reached my desk."

"We're still looking at these two," Grady put in. "We haven't gotten a complete picture, but we think they may have had a connection to us, but not for some years."

Lissa turned to Bertrand. "Do you know a man in your county named Robert Evers?"

Bert smiled. "Sure. Lives in Cabbottom in the western part of the county."

"Have you seen him lately?"

"No. Far as I know he hasn't come back from Montana yet.

Elk."

"Elk?"

"Time of year a lot of the boys head out there for Elk hunting. Evers usually goes out with his hunt club buddies for a month. Should be back soon. Do I get to ask 'why'?"

Grady took the question. "He used to work for us."

"Yeah. Lot of your people seem to find our part of the world when they retire."

"Any reason why?" Lissa asked.

"Well, I guess because even though everybody talks, nobody talks much to strangers. If you came looking for Evers, for instance, unless you came to me, prob'ly nobody'd know who you were talkin' about." His "good ole' boy" accent was accompanied by a sly smile.

After a moment, Lissa went on. Turning again to the whiteboard, she wrote:

Adrienne Jackson

Putting the marker down, she turned to the group. "Although we haven't yet turned up anything that points to the widow, she has always been there in our minds. We have a few lines out right now, and we hope to develop a better picture in a few days."

Grady was looking at the whiteboard. "Is there anything you can point to, Lissa, that says 'Adrienne'?"

"Only a feeling, I'm afraid, Mr. Grady. But there is something that isn't what it should be, in my mind."

"You'll have to bring me more than that, you know."

"I need a few more days. There is some information I'm developing that might be a reason." Lissa and Stan looked at each other. "There is a personal story I need to check out."

A PHONE CALL FROM SHERIFF BERTRAND told Lissa that Evers had returned from his hunting trip. Within minutes of receiving the call, she was on the phone with the retired agent.

"I hope you can help me with an inquiry," Lissa explained. "Are you on a secure phone?"

"It's digital," the man offered. "How secure that is, I don't know."

"Did you know Don Jackson?"

"Not in my department," Evers said.

"I can be in Mount Royal in about four hours. Can we meet?"

"I'm about ten minutes from there. Call me when you get to town." The connection clicked.

MOUNT ROYAL, VIRGINIA

PLEASED THAT HER CELL PHONE WORKED in the county seat, Lissa remained in her car while she called Evers' number. "I'm at the intersection where the blinking light is," she told the man. "Am I far from your place?"

"No. Just turn north on the main highway and head out of

town. When you get to Forked Creek, take the first left just over the bridge. Got that?"

"First left after Forked Creek. Is that a village?"

"Just a place. There's a store and then a bridge and the road on the left. Route 602."

"Ok. I take a left over the bridge onto 602?"

"Correct. Then go about a mile-and-a-half. There's a wide pull-off on the left, and a gravel road on the right. I'll be in an old green Jeep in the pull-off. I'll take you from there. Unless you have an old Jeep yourself."

"Afraid not. About ten minutes?"

"Yes."

"I'm on my way." Lissa closed the phone and made the turn at the blinking traffic light, then settled down for the run north. As she rolled along the valley road, the mountains rose on either side, giving her a sense of heading for a pass-through into another place. She came to a straight stretch along the Jackson River, and then the bridge. *I guess this is where the creek forks,* she thought, and slowed for the sharp turn to the left. Ignoring the odometer, she simply looked for the pull-off and the old green Jeep.

Bob Evers was a stocky, strong-looking man of perhaps seventy. His soft felt hat was a cross between a Westerner's and a backwoodsman's. He wore jeans and hiking boots and a flannel shirt, a leather vest his only concession to the Fall season. He stepped up to the car as Lissa pulled to a stop.

"Ms. King?"

"Mr. Evers." He opened the door for her, obviously not a

"new man," and waited while she gathered her leather shoulder bag.

A fast running stream separated the road from the flat valley. On the other side of the road a steep mountain rose to the north-west. The Jeep bounced and jumped from rock to rock on the rough-cut driveway leading to the top. It was all Lissa could do to keep from bumping into the door or the driver, so conversation waited until the vehicle came to rest in a clearing about a quarter of a mile up, but less than half-way to the top of the mountain. When the old Jeep at last stopped, Lissa sat for a second before saying, with a smile, "I see why you came to meet me."

"It keeps out most people." The tone of voice was a blend of smug and instructive.

"What a beautiful view." Lissa was standing in the yard, looking to the south over the valley she had crossed to get there. The mountains struck upward in every direction, leaving her feeling as if she were far, far from her own world. "It must be very quiet up here."

"Different. If you listen, there is a lot to be heard. Birds, deer, coyotes, even bear have something to say. I never get tired of listening."

They walked into the double-wide that dominated the small clearing. Inside it was cozy, a wood stove the central focus of the room.

"Coffee's hot," Evers said.

"Black, please," Lissa replied, opening her bag. From within she pulled pictures of Constantinescu and Lazarovici. When Evers handed her the coffee mug, she handed him the pictures. "Do you know these two?"

"This one," Evers indicated Constantinescu. "Not sure about the other. Might have had some contact with him a long time ago."

"Is Constantinescu working for us?"

"Did. But not after '85. We were on a different basis with his country by then. Why?"

"Did you hear about the death of a man named Don Jackson, here in the county? It was about three weeks ago."

"Yes. I saw it in the local paper when I was going through them last night. Catching up after being away is easy. The paper only comes out once a week." He smiled. "What's that to do with me? And Constantinescu?"

"Mr. Jackson worked for us. The facts in his death are not all that clear, and I'm looking at it for the agency."

"Grady still around?"

"My boss."

"He'll never leave, I suppose. Good man to have in that job."

"About Constantinescu: were you his handler?"

"That was my department, yes. Romania and Hungary both. But how does he figure in Jackson's story?"

"Constantinescu and Lazarovici were traveling on I-81 at the time Jackson died. They were at a rest stop a little later than what we believe is the time of death, and were interviewed in regard to an accident they might have witnessed a little earlier. The timing doesn't place them in Whitechapel, or even at the nearest exit from the interstate . . ."

"That would be the exit that would bring them west into the county?"

"Exactly. Anyway, Jackson had been in their part of the world only a week before he died, and the coincidence is too good to ignore."

"I don't remember any contact between my man and Jackson," Evers said, "but then, unless it was something significant, I might not have known. Who is the representative in Bucharest today?"

"I don't know. Would the information be there?" Lissa thought about her conversation with her friend at the embassy. She hadn't pursued the question from that angle.

"Worth a try."

"Romania and Hungary. I hadn't been thinking of that connection," Lissa said, almost to herself. "That's an interesting avenue."

"Interesting in what way?"

"Jackson's wife was Adrienne Toth. Her parent's came out of Hungary in '56, during the revolt."

"A lot of people came out then."

"Yes, but not many of them had a connection to the agency."

"You might be surprised," was all Evers said.

NORTHERN VIRGINIA

A SECURE PHONE CALL TO THE EMBASSY in Bucharest a day later brought a modest surprise: Jackson and Constantinescu had indeed been in contact about ten years earlier, the agency man reported. Constantinescu had been feeling out support for returning Transylvania to Hungary, an issue in which neither the agency nor the U.S. government had much interest. There the matter had rested. And that, according to Lissa's notes, was just about the time Adrienne and Don had met. *Could that play into the story of Jackson's death?*

WASHINGTON, D.C.

THE APPOINTMENT WAS FOR FIVE-THIRTY, and typically, Lissa was a few minutes early. She had to wait for Adrienne to open the door.

"Hello Mrs. Jackson."

"Ms. King, isn't it?" Adrienne was exhibiting an unbecoming vagueness, Lissa thought.

"That's right. May I come in?" The woman was still standing in the open doorway, as if she were confronting a vacuum cleaner salesman.

"Oh, yes. I'm sorry. Please come in." She turned and led the way down the short hall to the library. A low fire was burning in the grate.

"Do you have some news?"

"No. I'm afraid I have some more questions, instead."

"I don't know what else I can tell you," Adrienne said, her face clouding slightly.

"May I sit?"

"Oh, yes. How rude of me. I'm sorry." They had been standing in front of the fire. Adrienne sat to the right of the fireplace and indicated a matching chair on the other side of the hearth for Lissa.

"I do wish this would all be over," Adrienne sighed. She shook her head, as if to clear it of a memory, looked at the fire, and then, her gaze steadied by some inner thought, she looked at her visitor. She almost smiled. But not quite.

"What I wanted to look at with you," Lissa began, pulling some papers from her briefcase, "were the travel records I obtained from the passport office. I was looking particularly at your visits to Hungary over the last ten years."

"Why would that be of concern?"

"Well, because frankly, we are looking at everything connected with Mr. Jackson, looking to see if there is anything in the background we should know about. Your visits to Hungary fall into that category, since the two of you were there together in the last year. But perhaps you were not aware that eastern Europe was your husband's area of interest." Lissa stopped to give Adrienne a chance to respond.

"My parents," Adrienne said without elaboration.

Lissa said nothing. The silence held itself for a moment or two.

"My parents. They had gone back to retire there, you see."

"Of, course. They came out in '56, during the revolution, didn't they?"

"Yes. They were newlyweds then. So when things started to come apart, they made their way to Vienna, and eventually to America. But they never got over being homesick, I think."

"When did they return?"

"Oh, ten or twelve years ago. My father was ready to retire from his business, and things were opening up in Hungary. He decided to invest in the new economy."

"Was it a good investment?"

"Oh, yes. My father was a very good businessmen." Another long pause. "So naturally I wanted to visit them when I could."

"Did -- do you feel any pull to live there someday?" Lissa's question was off-hand.

"I hadn't given it any thought. They're both gone now, and like most Hungarians, we had more relatives in America than there." She smiled and looked at the fire.

"In your earlier trips to Hungary, did you do any traveling around, get to meet family you hadn't seen before? Any of that?"

"My trips were always educational for me. Yes, I still have relatives there, of course, and my parents were eager for me to meet them. Over the years I spent time with great aunts and uncles and a few cousins my age."

"How about after you and Don began to go there together? Was he introduced to the whole family?"

"Of course. Especially because I was older when we married. I think my parents and the rest of the family had given up on my ever getting married. We went there a couple of times before we were married."

"But you were married here, not there?"

"Yes. We made the decision on a Wednesday night, and were married on Friday morning. It was a very private ceremony. Before a judge I knew on the District court."

"I would think your parents were disappointed."

"No. Relieved, would better characterize their emotions." *That almost sounded like a joke*, Adrienne thought. *I hope I'm beginning to sound normal.*

The doorbell rang at that moment, and Adrienne broke off her reminiscence. Excusing herself, she left the room, closing the door gently behind her.

Lissa looked around. Such a contrast with the cabin. Where that was rough and dark and cozy, this room was all bright and warm in a different way. The walls were white, with gold accents on the bookcase trim. The furniture was old and of fine craftsmanship. Even the fireplace, black marble around the opening and on the hearth, brass screen, black and brass tools neatly standing by the opening, spoke of elegance and quality. *Two people, two worlds. Make that three: his, hers and her parents'.*

Lissa was aware of muffled voices on the other side of the door. It opened and Adrienne, accompanied by the young man Lissa had seen on her last visit to the apartment, came into the room.

"This is Mr. Arno, my graduate assistant."

"I believe I saw you the last time I was here. How are you Mr. Arno?" Lissa extended her hand. The return was less a grip than a slide.

A little sweaty. I wonder why?

"Since you're not a policeman, I guess I can't ask if you're harassing Mrs. Jackson, can I?" he said with a smile.

"Oh, but I am a sworn officer of the court, Mr. Arno. And I'm sure even international law recognizes that." She added a smile to the end of the sentence. "And no, I'm not harassing Mrs. Jackson. I'm just trying to complete our investigation. "

"Any questions I can answer?" His question was put less aggressively than his first one.

"Have you visited Hungary, Mr. Arno?" A shot in the dark, but those often pay off.

"Ahh. Not in many years, Ms. King."

So maybe there could be a connection. A speculation, not a question. *Another thing to look at.* "Well, I've asked what I needed to, Mrs. Jackson. If there is anything else, I'll call. Are you going to be back in your classroom this week?"

"Yes, I think so. It is time." She looked at Arno.

Obviously the box full of personal stuff we saw him carrying is back in her office, Lissa concluded. *I think I have some more searching to do at the passport office.* With that she said goodbye, and turned to the door. Before she left the room, she turned back to the two.

"Just one more question, Mrs. Jackson." She paused before going on: "Did you ever go hunting with your husband?"

Adrienne froze for just a micro-moment. "Yes, of course. We often went down during the fall hunting season."

"But not this year?"

"No. No, this year I was unable to find the time to get away."

"You have your own guns?"

"Yes."

"We didn't find any at the cabin other than a rifle."

"That was Don's. Mine have been at the gunsmith's for cleaning and checking since last season."

"Are they still there?"

"Yes." Going to the desk she opened a pigeon-hole drawer. Retrieving a business card, she turned and handed it to Lissa. "Here's the name of the man who has them."

"I see Mr. Kelley is in the county."

"Yes. He has been taking care of Don's guns, and mine, for a long time. A very good man."

Handing the card back to Adrienne, Lissa again wished the two a good morning, and left the apartment.

IN THE PARKING GARAGE Adrienne opened the heavy rear door of her Mercedes ML320. A canvas duffle bag, her AWOL bag, Don had called it, sat alone. Opening it, she checked to make sure her hiking boots and down jacket were in place. The bag also held jeans, a heavy shirt, and other necessities for a quick trip to Riversee. She and Don had been in the habit of keeping things they needed in their vehicles. Over the years the spontaneous "let's go to the cabin" moments had dwindled, but the bag had remained in the back of the SUV. Perhaps it was a reminder of a better time.

The weather was a help, Adrienne thought, as she turned out of the garage onto the avenue. Washington could offer warm, bright days even in early November, and the clear blue sky extended as far as she could see. Across the river to the west the day looked fine.

Instead of turning north, toward the university, she went south a few blocks, then turned to cross the river into Virginia. The early morning traffic on the Interstate had moderated, and she moved easily into the left lane, reserved during rush hour for vehicles with more than one occupant. As the road opened up, Adrienne used her cell phone to call her department. She would not be in today, she told the secretary. Something in connection with her late husband's affairs. *Not the best word to use,* she thought. She set the cruise control at a precise five miles an hour over the posted limit and headed west.

WHITE CHAPEL, VIRGINIA

THERE WAS STILL FROST ON THE SHADED GROUND around the cabin when Adrienne stepped out of her car. She stood for a moment before walking forward to the cabin. The sun was still rising behind the building. She shivered perceptibly as she stepped onto the shaded porch and opened the door. Taking her bag to the upstairs bedroom, she unpacked the hiking boots, jeans, shirt and down jacket, putting the clothes on the bed. The room was chilly, so she didn't linger as she changed from her city clothes. Stepping out onto the little balcony that was bathed in sunlight, she let the sun warm her.

Without building a fire in the fireplace, Adrienne left the cabin and walked up the path to the woods. In the shade of the great pines the ground was just losing the white of early morning. Leaves from the oaks and sugar maples had blown over the path, but the melting frost had robbed them of their crunchiness. It was quiet where she walked.

Adrienne stood for a long time, staring at the scuffed earth around the root that had caught Don's boot. She could still see the boot mark in the duff, but most of the disturbed earth now lay under fresh leaves. As the sun rose higher it penetrated the branches and began to warm the woman's shoulders. It seemed to her that only a moment had passed, but the moving sun told her that she had been standing there much longer. She had relived those hours of the day Don died. In her mind she could see Don coming around the turn in the trail, see him approach the all-too-visible root, hear the sound of the hammer hitting the cap on the shell, even smell the acrid telltale of gunpowder. And see her man sink to the ground. The picture was, in her mind, complete.

Adrienne backed slowly away from the edge of the path, turned and walked down the trail to the cabin.

Before going back inside she went to the car and retrieved a small bag containing coffee and bread. As she passed the kindling box on the porch she picked up a handful of the small sticks Don had so regularly collected and stored there. In the kitchen she turned on the water, ran it to purge the pipes, and then used the kindling to start a fire in the cookstove. While it heated, she put a pot of water on for coffee, then went to the small wood-fired hot water heater and used the remaining kindling to start that fire.

In the living room, by the fireplace, an old copper washtub with a lid held more kindling. Crumpling six pieces of newspaper from the basket on the other side of the fireplace, she placed a few sticks of kindling over them, and then three logs stacked like an "A" frame. She placed two more pieces of newspaper on top of the logs.

Still kneeling on the hearth, she picked up a "strike-anywhere" match, scratched it across one of the hearth stones, and reached in to light the paper on top. Don had taught her that trick years before, to preheat the chimney and help create a draft. As the paper flared and burned, she lit a second match and touched it to the paper at the base of the kindling. In a few seconds the flames took hold and a fire was soon crackling in the fireplace. Adrienne continued to kneel before the growing warmth, letting it soak into her bones. Only when the fire had grown too hot to be so close did she stand up and step back. She smiled at the success of her efforts, then began to cry softly. *Just building a good fire is a legacy from Don*, she thought.

THE SOUND OF THE COFFEE PERCOLATING on the stove brought her thoughts back to the present. There was another sound coming from outside. Standing, she turned to the door. A car was moving slowly toward the cabin. She realized with a start that it was Jason's old red sedan. She watched from inside as the car came to a stop beside her own. She stepped to the door, opened it, and walked out onto the porch. She remained in the shadow just under the deep roof.

"Why are you here?"

Jason said nothing. He walked the few yards to the bottom of the stairs. The sun was directly in his eyes, and so he squinted, using his hand as a sunshade.

"I had to talk to you. You did not come to your office, and you did not answer the phone, so I took a chance you would be here." His enunciation was more precise than ever.

"I've said all I had to say to you this morning. Is this about your thesis, your degree?"

"No."

"Then what?"

"About your late husband."

Adrienne turned and went back into the cabin. She glanced at the fire, then went into the kitchen and poured herself a cup of coffee. Standing at the sink, with her back to the window, she faced Jason, who had come as far as the doorway.

"What about Don?"

"Adrienne, I know where you were the morning he died."

"I was with you."

"Not until nine o'clock."

"Where, then, do you think I was?" Her hands remained closed around the hot cup. Only the warmth of the china kept them from feeling icy.

"You were here."

"Impossible."

"Not really."

"I could not have been here, and then at my office, could I?"

"I just drove down here, Adrienne. It took me less than three hours. And that old car of mine is no speedster."

"Go on." Her voice was without emotion, cold as her hands.

"Do you not know what your husband was doing?"

"Doing? Doing where? When? I don't know what you're talking about, Jason."

"What he did when he traveled to Europe."

"We never talked about his work. Most of the time I didn't even know where he was going."

"Why do you think I wanted to be your lover?" The words were harsh, edged.

"At first I didn't think about it, Jason."

"You mean it just 'happened'?"

"I thought so."

"And now?"

"I think you wanted to use me to assure your success at the university."

"To assure my success." Jason's lips curled into a sardonic smile. "My success, dear professor, does not depend on another set of letters after my name. I have, already, as many degrees as I can use."

For just a millisecond Adrienne's mind wrapped itself around the idea that Jason had pursued her because he found her irresistible, attractive, but the look on his face quickly wiped away that idea.

"A fit of unbridled passion, perhaps? You lost your head? I was too beautiful to ignore? Tell me Jason. Lie to me some more."

"No more lies, Adrienne. Time now for truth."

"Do you know the truth, Jason?"

"About you? Yes. About what happened to your husband? Yes. And so do you."

"I know nothing the police don't know, Jason, and I only know what they know."

"Not true. They, for instance, do not know how you made it happen." His voice was low, cunning. Not a thing changed in her face. Only her breath betrayed her anxiety, her fear.

"You are making something out of nothing, Jason. Do you really think I found you so captivating that I would kill for you?"

"That is exactly what you did."

"I wouldn't, and I couldn't, Jason. Certainly not for you. I am afraid you have too much imagination for international diplomacy. I can't believe I ever agreed to mentor you and your thesis. You are quite out of your mind. I'll review your status with Dr. Mays first thing tomorrow morning." She turned, and with her back to him, Adrienne stared out the window. She could not see what he was doing, but she heard the click of a latch. Turning, she saw that he had sprung a hidden lock on the side of the gun cabinet near the door to the livingroom. The side swung away, revealing a secret compartment between the studs in the wall. Jason turned to face her. He was holding a small bore shotgun. Adrienne's face paled in the strong light coming through the windows above the porch roof.

"How did you know about that?" Her voice for the first time betrayed emotion.

"You are perhaps too trusting, to leave keys to this place lying about. I have been here to look."

"Don built that cabinet." Her voice betrayed both admiration and surprise. Admiration for her late husband's cleverness, and surprise that Jason had found the secret. "He worried that anyone breaking in would have plenty of time to force open the door of the main cabinet without being disturbed."

"I thought your guns were at the gunsmith's."

Adrienne said nothing.

"Then what is this?" Jason thrust the small double-barreled shotgun forward, barrel toward her. Adrienne involuntarily put her hands before her face and turned.

"Don't. Don't point that at me."

"Is it loaded?"

"It doesn't matter. Jason, put it down." But the man continued to hold it, now with two hands, still toward her, but pointing to the ceiling.

"It's the one you used, isn't it?" Jason stated it as if it were a fact. "You were very clever, my dear."

"Stop it, Jason. Stop it and put that away and leave. Now." Her voice was constricted, controlled.

"I don't think I will leave, Adrienne, not now at least. We still have some things to talk about."

"What things? What is there left to say? Leave now and please get out of my life."

"Very cool, Adrienne. Very cool. How do you manage to stay so dispassionate? I don't recall such detachment in you except in public."

"Don't be a bastard, Jason. Don't! Do you want me to say 'I love you?' Too late for that. Too late for anything now."

"No, Adrienne. I don't want you to love me, I want you to

understand what you have done."

"I've done nothing."

"Then what is this gun hidden in your secret compartment? What about the gunsmith?"

"It was not at the gunsmiths. Only my rifle is there."

"Then if you have nothing to hide, why did you lie to that police woman?"

"She's not a police woman. And I told her that because I had to explain where the gun was, didn't I?"

"You can deny all you want, but the fact remains that we both know you killed Don. What some might not understand is why you did it." Jason's voice was low and almost caressing.

"Stop that, Jason." The man stepped forward, still holding the shotgun. "I didn't kill Don. I didn't." Adrienne reached out and grabbed the barrel. There was deafening 'boom' as the chambered shell discharged. "I didn't." Adrienne's face went from surprise to disbelief to dead, in the space of a few seconds. As she slid to the floor, her hand still around the barrel, Jason wrenched the gun from her grasp. He became aware of a new sound, and as he turned toward it, Lissa King and Stan Morris were coming through the door.

Still clutching the shotgun, Jason turned it toward the pair coming at him. Lissa, in the lead, continued non-stop as Jason's hand slid to the trigger. Stepping into him, Lissa reached forward and pushed the barrel higher into the air, at the same time using it as a lever to throw the man off balance. Her foot struck out and hooked his ankle, and he was on the floor, the gun harmlessly discharged into the ceiling. In a flash Morris was on top of him and the gun clattered to the floor.

From a Nugent holster clipped to her belt in the small of her back, Lissa drew her own gun, a snub-nosed .38 police special. Holding it to Jason's head she ordered him to turn face-own as Morris stood up. His hands behind his back, he lay quietly as handcuffs clicked around his wrists.

"Jason Arno," Stan Morris began, "I am arresting you in connection with the death of Adrienne Jackson. You have the right to remain silent, but anything you do say may be taken down and used in evidence against you." Standing over the man, Stan helped him to his feet. Arno stood facing the two officers.

"It was an accident," was all he said.

VERONA, VIRGINIA

IN THE REGIONAL JAIL Lieutenant Morris secured an interview room. Jason Arno sat across a small table. A microphone and video camera recorded their conversation. On the other side of a double glass wall, Lissa King watched, but did not participate. This was strictly a state case, but the federal agent wanted to hear anything the man might have to say about Adrienne and Don Jackson.

"I began an affair with Adrienne -- with Dr. Jackson -- about two years ago. We were, I think, attracted to each other because we both specialized in international law and, especially, Europe after the end of the Soviet era. I had come to the university for a Ph.D., and Dr. Jackson was the professor I most admired. When she invited me to apply for an assistantship in her department, I was very honored. I had been out of school for many years, as you can imagine, and I had feared a struggle to keep up. It wasn't difficult, however, and I found it easy to complete the academic work, the development of my thesis, and the duties as a teaching assistant."

"How would you describe your relationship with Dr. Jackson?"

"In the beginning it was strictly what you would call 'professional.' But sometime during the second year, when I was working more closely with her after class, we became -- more intimate." Jason was clearly uncomfortable with these revelations, but he continued on: "At first it was just getting to know each other better, discovering personal things we shared, or places we had in common."

"What 'places?'"

"We both had family in Eastern Europe, and had visited there over the years many times."

On the other side of the glass, Lissa sat up, her eyes wholly focused on Jason. She had not had time to look into the man's travel history. Perhaps there was something here that she could use.

"From that point we began to discuss more personal, more intimate things. Adrienne, it seemed to me, was not so much lonely as, how do you say it? Unfulfilled, yes that's it. Unfulfilled. I didn't think at first that she was interested in anything so compelling as an affair. I just felt she saw me as someone she could talk to without misunderstanding."

"Did you misunderstand her?"

"You mean did I discover that she really was looking for something more? Yes, I had not seen that at first, but over the next few months --"

"When was that?"

"About a year and a half ago. Anyway, we just moved from being professional associates to being friends to becoming lovers. But all the time I never felt that she didn't also love her husband. With us it was, I think, just passion. She was a very passionate woman." There was a certain smugness in that description.

"Did she tell her husband?"

"My god, no! She was such a private person. I think she would never have told anyone, even long after her husband's death. This was just a sort of aberration. I think maybe the only time since she was married that she had a lover. In fact I'm certain."

"Now tell me about this morning." Morris shifted in his chair, leaning forward, toward Arno.

"Early this morning I came to the conclusion that she was no longer interested in me, and I, frankly, was just tired of the relationship. She had made it too demanding. I told her I was leaving, and she took it to mean what I wanted it to: leaving her. She didn't sound that unhappy, herself. Perhaps she had realized what she had done, and wanted to put distance between us. Anyway, she told me that I was not only to leave her bed, you understand, but to leave her office at the university as well; that she had already taken steps to have my assistantship transferred to another member of the faculty. She said it was time, and I agreed."

"So you were the one who initiated the break-up?"

"I would characterize it that way, yes."

Lawyers sound the same whether they are local or international, Stan thought. "Were you upset at all?"

"You mean enough to kill her? But why would I want to do

102

that? I tell you that I was ready to end the affair. In fact, I was not the one who started it, or who drove it." Jason continued to speak calmly and with a slightly bemused expression on his face. "Whatever happened between us was over, and it was time. I think it was time even if her husband had not died."

"Tell me about this morning. Why did you follow her to Riversee?"

"Truthfully? I was worried when I knew she had called in to take the day off. I tried her home and no one answered. I thought the death of her husband might make her --- well, might lead her to do something to herself."

"Did you think she was responsible for Don Jackson's death?"

"I am convinced of it."

"Tell me about the hidden gun. How did you find out about it?"

"Adrienne had once mentioned that her husband was a very clever man, with his hands as well as his mind. She told me he was fascinated with secret compartments and had read a lot about them. I knew she had guns. She had told me about hunting with her husband. So it wasn't difficult for me to think about where to look and how to find such a compartment, you see?"

"But you didn't just find it this morning, did you?"

"No. I admit that I had visited the cabin about six months ago. She had left her keys in my apartment. You know how that can be?" A hint of a conspiratorial smile crossed his face. "I had some time, and I knew her husband was away, so she wouldn't miss them. I prowled around until I found the catch on the side of the wall. He had disguised it to look like a coat hook, but it didn't seem the right place for one. I pulled it, and the side of the cabinet opened."

"Were the guns in there?"

"Sure. Hers and his. They put them there when they would not be back for a while."

Stan wrote briefly on the yellow pad in front of him, adding to notes he had been making during the interview. "How long ago was that?"

"Last spring. Her husband was on one of his 'business trips'."

Leaning forward in the darkened room, Lissa said in a whisper, "Ask him if he knew what Don's business was." It was the first question she had fed into the earpiece Stan was wearing.

"Did you know what Mr. Jackson's work was?"

"I assumed he was in some intelligence work. She never told me, but from things she didn't say, I knew that. You know?"

Stan didn't answer, but continued to look at Jason. The other man did not look away.

After a long pause, Jason shifted his position in his chair and leaned toward Morris. "Look, Lieutenant, I'm not a criminal lawyer, but I don't think you can make a solid case for murder. I admit that I was holding the shotgun, and that it went off while I was holding it, but Adrienne had grabbed it and in the struggle it discharged. I had no reason to kill her, certainly no reason to even want her out of my life any more than she herself wanted it. I'm telling you about our relationship, about how it was between us, not to justify her death, but simply to explain how it was. I know you are looking for a killer, but so was I. When I pulled that gun out of the cabinet, I had no idea it was loaded. It was to confront her, to make her understand that I knew she had lied to the security agent, King. I am sure she killed her husband, but it was not because of me."

Lissa was sitting back against her chair now, away from the window, trying to move away from the accusation Jason was making. She and Stan had slipped into the house just in time to hear Jason accuse Adrienne of Don's murder, and to see the woman reach for the gun. It had all happened so quickly that neither she nor Stan had moved fast enough. It was, she was sure, going to end with Jason being charged with nothing more than involuntary manslaughter.

ROANOKE, VIRGINIA

WHAT I'D LIKE TO KNOW," Stan said, "was where you got that .38. The blued steel and plain wooden grips look like a government issue from at least 1950. I didn't realize the feds were in such dire straits that they couldn't afford to issue Glocks or Berettas." The two were in Stan's livingroom. The house was gracious in size, but sparsely furnished. It had an almost institutional feel: a leather sofa, a blocky modern end table on either side, one easy chair, also leather, a coffee table and a side chair that looked as if they had come from the same office furniture catalog. A reading lamp beside the easy chair and a non-descript floor lamp at one corner of the sofa illuminated the otherwise shadowed room. They had finished the paperwork related to Jason's arrest, then come down to Stan's office in the city 80 miles south of Whitechapel. Having finished work he had to do regarding the case, Stan had taken Lissa to dinner at a local pub, then on to his house.

"The gun? Actually it was my father's. I do have an issue

9mm, but I carry the .38 as a backup. Today I hadn't put on my shoulder holster because I wasn't really expecting to engage anyone at the cabin. Besides," she grinned, "I had you with me."

"That holster looks like the kind the bureau used to issue a long time ago. Was your dad ever FBI?"

"No. Always 'the agency.'"

"You told me he was dead, I know, but had he retired before he died?"

Lissa's face, in the low light of the room, wasn't easy to read. Stan saw only a brief flash of pain and then it was gone, replaced by a different light; one he couldn't read.

"My father died on the job, Stan, on a mission."

"Do you know what happened?"

"I think so. At least I've had a long time to work it out, and yes, now I'm sure I know."

"It wasn't clean?"

"It was an operation in Romania. Something went wrong, and my father got caught. There was a fight, and he died."

"How did you get the gun, then? Had he left it at home?"

"According to his partner, Father had given it to him when things looked bad, because the other man had lost his own weapon."

"But he had another one?"

"Both did. Or were supposed to." A long silence, and then the woman continued: "It was one of those ops where things were not entirely clear. Who was the good guy and who was the bad one.

My father had set things up, trying to bring a double agent out into the open, hoping to plug a major hole in the box. Too many other people were involved, I believe, and so it didn't go down as planned. Near the border, almost in sight of his exit hole, there was a firefight and, according to his partner, my father held back to secure the location."

"And he needed his backup gun?"

"And he needed his backup, yes. But his partner had it."

"The partner made it back, then."

"Yes."

"Was there an investigation?"

"Of course. It was one of Grady's first as chief of the internal security section."

"And all was as it seemed?"

"That was the conclusion. Grady told me, much later, that it was as much because there was no evidence to the contrary, and no hope of getting any."

"Is that what you wanted to do when you joined?"

"Yes."

"Is that why you had such well developed contacts at the embassy? Had you taken a second look?"

"After I had been in the department for about three years I began looking around whenever I had the time. I went over the records of course, early on, but as I gained experience and learned some of the things Grady could teach me, I started going deeper. And then, of course, everything opened up, and the Romanians were our friends, and a lot of records became available, declassified and opened. That's when I started building a case."

"Was there one?"

"Oh, yes. A very substantial one. There were connections between him, his partner, and their counterparts over there. A couple were still alive. Are still alive," she corrected herself.

"And you believe something went on that shouldn't have?"

"The partner and his wife had a lot of connections there, and in the surrounding countries. I am sure that they were working both sides, and my father rumbled them. I believe that is why he was caught, and why he died."

"Did you show your case to Grady?"

"No. By then I don't think anybody cared or wanted to know. It was all over."

"So the partner stayed on, and nothing happened?"

"His partner was Don Jackson." The whispered words hung in the air. Lissa said nothing more.

Stan sat forward on the sofa. He turned to look at Lissa. Her face was quiet, composed, blank.

"Oh, Lissa," was all the man could say.

After what seemed like the longest, most desperate silence he had ever heard, Stan turned to look at the woman beside him. Lissa's face was composed, untroubled. "I will have to take this to my chief," Stan said.

"No. I'll take it to Grady, myself, Stan. Please."

"Now?"

"In the morning, Stan. Can we do that?" The cell phone in her purse began to beep. For a moment the two looked at each other, trying to read the future. Finally Lissa reached in and retrieved the tiny electronic connection to her own world. Looking at the caller ID, she flipped the cover and said, "Yes Mr. Grady?"

"I heard about your day. I've also seen the report from the state police, and the transcript of the interview."

"I'm sorry it played out the way it did."

"I also had a call from Evers."

"Yes. I saw him."

"He wanted to know if your father had been with the agency. I told him 'yes.' I must be getting close to retirement, King. I failed to put the two together. Your father and Jackson."   Lissa said nothing, but looked at Stan.

"I'll be coming in tomorrow, Mr. Grady."

"Better make it early. There will be a lot to do."

"Lieutenant Morris will bring me."

"Is he with you now?"

"Yes."

"Let me talk to him."

Lissa handed the phone to Stan.

"You been following this conversation, Morris?"

"We've covered it all, Grady."

"For now, I want you to keep this to yourself. This is an internal matter until I say otherwise. Understood?"

Before Morris could respond, the phone went dead. Handing it back to Lissa, he sat back against the cushions. He looked at his other hand, still holding the holstered .38. Getting up, he walked to a small gun safe. "I'll just put this in here for now, Lissa." After locking the compartment, he turned to look at her. She looked so calm he had a hard time adjusting the image to the reality. It was going to be a long night.

NORTHERN VIRGINIA

"I DON'T HAVE TO EXPLAIN," Grady began, "but you should know that in the end, the agency is rid of a rogue agent under circumstances that are best buried with the man." Morris was sitting in Grady's dimly lit offices at the end of a long, and for him, an unpleasant day. "I am also without one of the best investigators I've ever had."

Stan sat forward.

"Lissa, at my suggestion, has been allowed to resign and is no longer with this organization."

"Where is she, Grady?"

"At home, I suppose. Not one of mine to worry about now."

"You're certain she made the accident happen?"

"In her own words, Lieutenant. She hadn't counted on such an early discovery. That and a little early morning frost preserved enough evidence to make it possible for the autopsy to provide us with the first hard clue. When I reviewed the reports from your visits to the cabin I saw a pattern, but I was reluctant to act on it."

"Pattern?"

"You haven't been to the schools we teach. It was almost a textbook plan for making a kill look accidental."

"Did you know her father?"

"That was the missing piece, you see. I was not in the security side at that time, so there were agents and actions I wasn't aware of. King was one of them. I knew that Lissa's father had been with the agency in the past, but that was only a line in her background check. An important one, it turns out."

"So now what?"

"Well, as far as we are concerned, there is no story. It is over and buried with Jackson."

"I'm not sure I can do that so easily."

"From our perspective you'll have to. What you do personally is up to you, of course, but I advise you to keep it personal. You'll get no support from this agency. None."

AT THE JUNE GRADUATION EXERCISES at the university, the graduate degrees were handed out soon after the last speaker had retired to the row of chairs on the outdoor stage. Doctoral candidate Jason Arno was the second new doctor of philosophy to cross the white platform. He had survived the brief encounter with the state of Virginia, and as he had predicted, the state had found no case. He had returned to the university, quietly stepped away from his assistantship, and finished his dissertation. Now he was taking the final steps. As he reached the grass and gravel walkway and looked around, he was surprised to see a pair of men in dark suits blocking his way.

"Janos Arcos?" said one. He flashed a shield. "Immigration and Naturalization Service. We've been wanting to talk to you."

ACROSS THE RIVER IN ALEXANDRIA, Stan Morris picked up the two suitcases and loaded them into his car. Lissa King, dressed comfortably for travel, locked the front door, put the keys in her purse, and turned to the street. Stan saw the weariness in her eyes. The simple act of locking her door had flashed a lifetime of emotion across her face. The careful, studied control was briefly shut down. His heart absorbed some of the heaviness he knew she carried in her own.

"Do you have any idea of when you'll be back?"

"No, Stan. I've rented out the house for six months, and they may want it longer. I'm planning on at least that long." Lissa walked deliberately down the short brick staircase, turned, looked for a moment at the house, the home and the past she was leaving. She turned slowly to Stan, gave him a quick smile, and got into the car.

IN FRONT OF THE INTERNATIONAL DEPARTURES TERMINAL Lissa stood at the open door of Stan's car. A sky cap had taken her luggage, leaving her momentarily relieved of all responsibility. As she closed the door she bent and put her head through the open window. "I don't know where I'll end up, Stan. Or when I will be back. I'm sorry."

"I'll be here to pick you up, Lissa," was all he said.

Lissa withdrew, turned and walked toward the doors to her future.

Everywhere I Go, There I Am

Not all things criminal begin with criminal intent. Sometimes it just works out that way. In this story, a man comes face-to-face with a person whom he invented, and discovers himself.

THE WHIRR OF THE TAPE RECORDER REWINDING slowed and stopped. A "click" as the play button was pushed, and then the voice began. It was a very professional voice, and the listener was aware, from time to time, that its owner used it much like an instrument. It was almost theater.

I WALKED INTO THE GENERAL STORE anchoring the small strip of businesses, looked around at the counters and bins of local produce, the cooler with its cans of soft drinks, and the refrigerator with its six-packs of cheap beer, and I knew I was home. Not my home, but a home I could construct from what was around me in the little town of Millville.

The town itself is small, busy with local people doing whatever they do in small towns today, which isn't much, but they do it with a fervor and intensity born of pleasure in being where they are, doing what they do. It is not a hard place to find, but it can be a difficult place to love. It can also be a great place for someone like me to make a difference.

In this store a man can find locally grown potatoes as well as boots, nails, even lottery tickets. It is across the street from the courthouse and the bank. The main street cuts the county in two, running east to west. Another highway crosses it north and south, but the four quadrants don't represent a natural division of the community. The mountains do. And then there are the people.

We came here, my wife Ella Kate and I, to take up a small charge in a chapel long supported by the community, though not a mainstream denomination. We came because, as I told the search committee, I'm getting older, looking for a quiet few years where I could plan a decent retirement, and where I would feel at home. I guess they never expected me to accept the relatively small salary, but the whole picture appealed to me, right down to the old manse next to the frame church. Here, I told Ella Kate, we could be what we really are at heart: small town people, country people, members of a family. Ella Kate agreed it was what she'd wanted for us from the beginning. But that was a long time ago.

When I was a boy, back in Montana, I learned to love the mountains and the small, quiet ways of the people. I could have stayed there, I suppose, but I was ambitious; eager to make something more of myself. I wanted to be the person I imagined myself to be: smart, clever, able to convince others of things I believed. Preaching, I discovered, was a calling I understood. Standing on the platform of a Sunday afternoon, after the others had left the sanctuary, I could hear myself preaching, see the congregation listening, nodding approval, giving me back that wonderful emanation of love and respect they had just given so eagerly to Reverend Friend and the choir and the lay leaders. It was a prideful conceit, I guess, and I would have a hard time, in the years just ahead, overcoming that. I would need to though, if I were going to lead such a congregation myself one day. And I did. No one knows how difficult that struggle was.

The Millville search committee was headed by Donald Tolliver. Donald is a tall, imposing gentleman of about 70, a long-time resident of the county, though not a native. Two other members of the congregation were part of the committee, but it was Donald who led them. A businessman with many interests in and out of the county, he was a major contributor to the church, and in some ways, feared by the other members. Not because he was threatening I realized, but because he had the money to give and held it as a sort of sword over the operation of the church. Working with a man like that, for the good of the community, could be a real challenge. It was the kind of situation I enjoyed. I think you'll understand why by the time I'm finished with my story.

Another member of the committee had come from Mississippi when she married her soldier-boy and moved to his home at the end of the war. The Second World War, that is. Around here "The War" can still mean the one fought in 1861. No, Amelia was elderly, but not that old. She had grown up in a city, and so her view of the local population . . . any country population for that matter . . . was that they were all just a little bit less sophisticated, less worldly than she, and therefore she was someone to whom others should listen. I always thought she felt somewhat put out at being only a member and not the chair of the search committee. She accepted her "place," seemingly without rancor, but I could sense it.

The other member was a farmer, a descendant of the family that had founded the church in the late 18th century. Elmo was not the most vocal, but a rather quiet, methodical man who listened carefully, considered what he heard, and in the end asked questions that were very good, very penetrating, very . . . dangerous?

"I'm real impressed with your background, Reverend. But I have to ask you what I think all of us want to know."

"Go ahead." I knew the question already. I wasn't uncomfortable with it, because it was one I would have asked in his place.

"Well, you've told us about your last three churches, all in big cities, and you've told us about going to college and then to a school of divinity." He shuffled the papers I had handed out at the beginning."Eastern Union Seminary, was it?" I nodded. "Pretty high powered for a man in a church with only a couple of dozen families, wouldn't you say?" I agreed, because on the face of it, how could I not? "Then why in the world would you want to come to our little church, with no affiliation, and with very little money to pay you? Surely you've done better. Could do better?"

I leaned in toward the three of them, sitting on the other side of the long refectory table. I smiled, I adjusted my position, I gave them all a slow appraisal, and nodded. "Fair question, Mr. Marshall. Absolutely one I would expect you to ask." I relaxed, sat back, smiled again.

"Well, then?" Amelia smiled at me, her head turned just so, to present a quizzical, but what she hoped was a penetrating look.

"I'm getting on in years now," I began (though I'm only in my 50s and all three of these people are at least 70 and more). Elmo I took to be about 75, and Amelia is I know for a fact over 80. "Well, let me put it this way." Now I sat forward again, gathering them in as it were, as they leaned closer to each other and toward me, to hear what I had to say. "I'm getting older, and it's time to find a place to finish up. To put down my last roots, I guess you'd say, and make myself ready for the final call. Oh, I'm not sick or anything (I could sense their question), but I've been working since I was a boy. I started out preaching when I was still a teenager, and I think I've done the Lord's work well." (Had to be careful here. Didn't want to sound conceited.) "It's time my wife and I settled down to stay. You know how a preacher's life is: always moving from church to church, town to town, following the way that opens. Answering the call that only you can hear." I paused, looked at them. "No, I guess you wouldn't know how that feels. You folks are firmly attached to where you started. We're not. My wife and I have lived in small towns and large cities and in more states than I can sometimes recall. But this town, this county, feels like home."

"And the money we can offer?" Donald Tolliver had been quiet for too long, I could tell. He wanted to assert his leadership and business acumen now. "We aren't going to come up with more, not now and probably not for a long time, unless you build a bigger congregation." There it was: "unless you build," the emotional connection I was looking for. Tolliver had already decided to hire me.

"We're okay about money, Mr. Tolliver. We've done fine in other larger, well funded congregations, and we both have money from our parents that has come to us. We own a few properties in Montana, and one in Illinois, and another one in Arizona, and they provide sufficient income that we can feel comfortable with whatever the congregation can afford. Within reason," I added. I waited a moment and then, like a fan unfolding, we all sat back in our chairs. I let the words fall into place in the minds of my interlocutors. The job was mine.

LIFE IN THIS SMALL, ISOLATED COMMUNITY WAS EVERYTHING I could ask for. The scenery was breathtaking, the climate moderate, the people . . . what can I say about the people? All seemed welcoming, certainly in the congregation. I knew I had the three members of the committee to thank for that, especially at the beginning, and I prayed that they would become my friends, not just my overseers. I wanted these people to accept what I could bring them: the Word, the understanding, the help in their times of trouble, and their helper in times of need. I wanted to be a real part of a real community.

Country people, you know, have so much more to give than city people. They are trusting, and want you to be a part of the world they open to you when you give them the chance, because that is what they have been doing all their lives. These are good people, honest people, who will accept you if you show them you are sincere, and I can do that very well.

I'm sure there were others, right from the beginning, who wondered about my coming to their community, and of course there is always someone who voices that question of "why here," but Donald and Amelia and even old Elmo were quick to defend their decision, as I knew they would be. Without being specific for instance, I knew that the elderly Mr. Marshall appreciated my position of relative personal wealth so that I didn't expect more from the congregation's limited resources. Amelia, too, nodded wisely whenever people asked about me, and affirmed that the church was lucky to have a man secure enough to accept a place in such a small congregation. Donald Tolliver was a city man. He had lived among these people a long time, but he was still an outsider in many ways. Respected for his wealth and power (he still had business in Atlanta and Washington), people figured if I could pass his scrutiny I was okay. It was an easy transition from our last church, the one in Oklahoma. I didn't have any trouble moving from a Sunday service for 500 to one for 50, or even 30. And I felt their approval, their love coming back to me as I stood before them on a Sunday morning, or the Tuesday bible study or, soon enough, a funeral for one of our own. I quickly found what they wanted to hear in my sermons, for instance: a biblical connection to today's times of trouble and pain was always a good theme. And hope for the sick and for the misdirected could always find heads nodding in agreement. I tried not to bore them, not to put them to sleep, and very much in my own way, to bring them some new insight into their own problems, their own way of dealing with their private and personal family lives and problems. And I loved the weddings! There weren't many, because there weren't too many young people in the community. The community was mostly retired people: farmers, parents with children living away from home, always with the promise that someday they would find a way to come back. Always a longing among my flock for times past. I could relate their lives to the difficult and joyous and confused lives of those in the bible, of course, and try to find some connection to today's world. I looked forward to my Sundays more than I had in years.

The work wasn't hard. Even preparing a sermon each week was a happy challenge. There were so many published ones in the church office from pastors of long ago that I could rewrite, and of course the internet, a strong presence even in this part of the world, offered other opportunities to find inspiration that could be downloaded. It's surprising how easy it is to cast thoughts in ways that are so universal that the people in the audience feel as if you are speaking to them directly.

THE FIRST HINT OF TROUBLE CAME ON A SATURDAY MORNING. Ella Kate brought the phone into my study. Handing me the cordless receiver, she mouthed "Tolliver," and smiled. I smiled in return.

"Hello, Donald." By now we were on an easy first-name basis. "Beautiful day the Lord has provided, isn't it?"

"I hope so, Davis. In fact I'm sure it will be." That was the first hint.

The tension in his words allowed me to seize the conversation: "What's troubling you, my friend?" I've always felt it more effective to project omniscience whenever possible. It's a technique that puts people in a cooperative frame of mind.

"Davis, can I come by and talk to you?"

I assured him that my door was always open to him, as to any member of the congregation, but especially to him. He said he was on his way, and hung up.

Now a minister, regardless of his congregation's size or age or makeup is always prepared to hear trouble, either about the congregant or about someone in that person's life. But I sensed in Donald's voice that his concern involved something more. It involved me.

"I don't know how to begin this," Donald said, walking in the door a few minutes later. His face was troubled. "But I felt you had to know."

"Are you okay, Donald? Nothing wrong with Susan, is there?" It was important he sense that my first concern was for his well-being. "Sit down," I said, putting my hand on his shoulder and walking him to the easy chair beside my desk, "Sit down and tell me what's on your mind. I can see you are troubled, my friend." He sat, settling himself as though he carried a weight he could hardly bear. I turned my swivel chair to face him and sat down, our knees almost touching.

"I received a letter this morning, and before I go further, I want you to understand that what distresses me is not the letter, not its contents, but that it is un-signed. Well, it's signed, but not with a name."

"Then how do you know who sent it?"

"I don't."

"It's anonymous?"

"Yes."

I laughed. "Well, then, Donald, let me guess: it's about me."

"You've already heard about it from someone else?"

"Not exactly. But it's happened before. Before I came here."

"It says you're not really a preacher." Donald's voice was quiet and flat. There was already doubt in it.

"Yes. That would be 'A Friend,' who signed it, wouldn't it?"

"That's right. That's what it says."

"You have to wonder whose friend, don't you?" I smiled. I hoped it was a reassuring smile. I couldn't tell.

"The letter says you never went to divinity school, that you were never ordained, and that you are stealing money from the church by pretending to be something you're not."

"Do you believe that, Donald? Am I not the preacher you and Amelia and Elmo hired?"

"I think you are."

"Well, then?"

"Why would someone send me this letter? You say you've seen it before, but what does that mean?"

"Donald, my friend, let me try to help you understand what it's like to be in the public eye." I bowed my head for a moment, trying to work out the best way to explain what was happening.

Before I could answer, Donald stood up, his six-and-half foot frame towering over me. This time it was his hand on my shoulder.

"Son, you don't need to tell me about being in the public eye. I've been there; still am in a way. I know how people can be. If you say this is nothing, and that there is no reason for me to believe what the letter says, that's good enough for me. You're doing a fine job in this little church, and I for one want you to keep on doing it." I looked up at my friend. His face told me about his honesty and his trust in me, and I was nearly reduced to tears.

WAS THERE SOME VEIL BETWEEN US? The congregation seemed as full as ever, the faces as friendly, but there was something emanating from them, I thought. Or was it just me? Were things from the past breaking into the world we had created here in Millville? I couldn't tell. My sermon was heard with what seemed to me a little less attention, the faces looked a little less focused on the inner light I was trying to kindle, but was that really in them, or in me? I couldn't tell.

The fellowship hour was noisy, with the usual laughter and voices raised in pleasure at friends meeting after a week of hard work. The table in the fellowship hall, where sweets and treats were spread across the wide white cloth seemed just as inviting and tempting as ever, but were they watching me? Were the members of my congregation as friendly, or was there a wariness? I'd been here for almost two years, and still there were some who considered me a stranger, and most all considered me an outsider. The difference was usually less palpable, more honest. Were some of the others sharing the anonymous letters? I thought I could feel less warmth and even strength in the hugs and handshakes that had followed the end of the service that morning.

I had been there long enough that when I preached a funeral service, for instance, I no longer had to say things like "I didn't know our brother, but he certainly made himself known in the community." Even the most private people are candid with their preacher, I think. Especially if they sense your interest is genuine. From the very first days among this congregation I let them know I listened without judging, judged without censuring, censured with understanding of man's fallibility. But it was a delicate balance to maintain, between shepherd and flock.

I stood in my usual place beside the door leading to the fellowship hall, greeting each of my congregation as they came through. There were smiles, and comments like "good sermon, Reverend," and "Enjoyed your service today, preacher;" the usual comments one hears and accepts much as we do "good morning" or "how've ya been," when we meet on the street. Of course there is a sincerity in all of that, in all of us, but there is a degree, if you know what I mean. We mean what we say, but there isn't as much "heart" in it perhaps, as when we are really concerned for a friend's well-being.

I was sure I knew who had received the letters. In the past it had been people like Donald and Elmo and Amelia, but other members of the church's leadership would have also been on the list. And always a lawyer who advised the board of governors when they needed it. Mostly, of course, they took their advice from prayer, and usually I was the one who helped them direct those prayers when they needed it. I wasn't always successful, but it worked most of the time. In a way it is the part of being a preacher I most enjoy.

"REVEREND ARMSTRONG, THIS IS EUGENA FLOWERS."

"Good morning, Mrs. Flowers. How are you on this beautiful day?"

"Not so good, Reverend. It's raining and too chilly for my rheumatism by half." The voice of the church board's chairman was almost as chilly as the late May morning.

"Still, the Lord has given it to us to do with as we will, and I'm always thankful for that."

"Then you'll understand, Reverend, when I ask you to meet with the board this evening, won't you?"

"Ah. You've received a letter, too."

"Yes. And not just me. So the board has decided to ask you to come to tonight's meeting."

"Of course, Mrs. Flowers. What time?"

"Six. And Reverend, please bring whatever you have that will support your ordination."

"God bless you," I said, as she hung up at her end.

Eugena, still "Mrs. Flowers" to me, had never been a negative or a positive in my time with the church, nor had she ever given me any reason to think she didn't trust me to do what was right. I knew that, as chair of the board, she had not cast a vote one way or the other on the question of hiring me, but she was not a firm supporter, either. I would have to focus my presentation tonight on her, that much was clear.

I spent most of the day preparing for the meeting. From a box I kept in the storage closet in my office I withdrew a file envelope made of heavy paper; the kind used to store legal documents. From it I removed several diplomas, including one that carried the seal of Eastern Union University, and the sub-head identifying it as coming from the divinity school. I held the parchment-like paper to the light of the window. I never tired of reading the Latin text below the seal. Roughly translated, the words proclaimed that Davis Lee Armstrong, having met all the requirements thereof, was hereby awarded the degree of doctor of philosophy, and was therefore entitled to all the rights and privileges thereof. I loved to read that aloud, loved the sound of the Latin words I could pronounce with ease and fluency. It was almost a second language to me, one of the first indicators that I could learn anything if I really wanted to. With only a little help from a teacher in the high school I had attended, I learned to read and write and speak this nearly dead language when I was in my teens. It has stood me in good stead all my life.

I put the diploma aside, drew out a rather thick manuscript, and placed it beside the diploma. The top page announced that it was a graduate thesis written by Davis Lee Armstrong, Candidate for the Degree of Doctor of Philosophy, and so on. A circular time/date stamp indicated that it had been received at 9:43 A.M., February 12th, 2003, by the theological seminary at Eastern Union University.

To the two documents, I added a letter from the president of the congregation in my last church, thanking me for my service to the community, and my leadership as pastor in the Church of the Shepherd and Disciples. I was proud of that letter, because it underlined how much growth I had encouraged, how many new members the church had when I left it, and the many community programs I had initiated. I studied it for several minutes before adding it to the package I was preparing. I had read it many times. I hoped that no one would notice or pay attention to the slight smudge that seemed to hover over the date and the address block on the creamy white paper. Too much handling would explain that, I thought.

I added a few more letters, and diplomas from the other university and college programs listed on my resume, put all of it in a large manila envelope, and sat back to give some thought and prayer to the up-coming interview.

THE MEETING WAS CONVENED in the fellowship hall of the church. For the size of the congregation the room was adequate, though one of the plans I had developed since coming here was to enlarge the "new" addition that had been made in 1957 or so. I held that the congregation couldn't continue to grow if newcomers and visitors felt we were as many as the building could handle. It is my belief that people don't want to participate in a place where they feel crowded any more than they do in a place where they feel overwhelmed by emptiness. This little church could easily hold a hundred worshipers, but fifty was about the limit for any social activity. I had overseen the initiation of a fund for expansion, had met with church developers and brought them to the church to talk to the members, and we were beginning a campaign to raise the funds. I even had encouraged the initiation of a matching grant from one of the founding families who still kept land in the county, though no one in the family still lived on it. There was already a fund of $50-thousand in the bank to get started. I admit that we, Ella Kate and I, hoped that the growth of the church would lead to a growth in my income, but at the moment that wasn't really uppermost in our minds. Seeing the church survive was our goal.

The meeting began with a prayer for guidance and a lot of apologies from the board of governors for even having to do what we were doing. Eugena didn't smile, however, when she asked me to answer the questions the letters had raised. I smiled, and said how sorry I was that the board had to deal with such terrible calumnies (I noted the searching looks from several of the members when I used that word), and instead of going directly to the questions, asked that they remember where we were in terms of growth and community participation compared with the congregation I had found when I arrived.

"I don't know how to explain why someone would send out the letters you have received or read. I can only tell you that there are people out there who have spent their lives in misdirected anger that results in this kind of behavior. As part of my preparation for the ministry I read a lot of psychology. I know that there are people in the world who believe it is their mission in life to bring others down, to disrupt real, honest lives, with accusations hiding behind anonymity and innuendo. It is hard to deal with people like that, hard to know whom you may have converted into a personal enemy, but I can assure you that there are people out in the wide world who will do these things." Did I make sense to these people? Were they following what I was saying? I thought so.

"Here," I continued, picking up the envelope I had prepared, "I believe you will find enough documentation to answer your questions." I stood and handed the package to Mrs. Flowers. I remained standing while she opened it and pulled out the contents.

"What do we have here, Reverend?" She was looking at the dissertation.

"That is the final draft of my doctoral thesis, as it was submitted to the committee at the university. I don't have a bound copy, but that will show you the amount of work I had to do to receive the degree that is attested to on the diploma."

Eugena started the manuscript on its journey around the table, passing it to Amelia, who sat next to her. Then she picked up the parchment attesting to my being a doctor of philosophy. Holding it for me to see, she pulled it back, looked at it again, then sent it on its way, following the thesis. "And that's what this is about, I take it?"

"Yes. My diploma. I'm extremely proud of that piece of paper. It represents a lot of work; more than just the dissertation." I

127

<u>was</u> proud of it, too. It hadn't been easy to obtain. Now I felt as if I were going to be called upon to defend it in front of this board of examiners.

"As well you should be, Reverend. I taught at the community college over in the valley, and I know what it means to earn one." She smiled, but behind the smile, I knew, was the mouth of a bull dog. She was not someone you could fool with a piece of paper and a few words.

The other documents were handed round, then returned to Mrs. Flowers. Amelia looked at me, looked at Eugena, but said nothing. It was Donald who broke the silence.

"I can't see any reason to prolong this, Eugena. Everything on the table is as Reverend told us at the beginning. I don't think we should let this go any further." His forceful voice held all the conviction necessary to see me past this hurdle.

"Lord," I began, "let thy countenance shine on those of us gathered here, and deliver us from the temptations of calumny, envy and falsehood. Let these good people find assurance in your word, and in your arms. Amen." For a moment no one moved. Then the others pushed their chairs away from the table and stood. I remained seated, my head down, my hands clasped, resting on the documents again gathered before me. I made plain my feelings as I relaxed at the touch of Donald's hand on my shoulder, the pats and pressing from the other members of the board. They left the room, saying nothing. All except Eugena Flowers.

"I just hope you are telling us the whole truth, Reverend." She turned away and walked out of the room. I sat for a minute or two more, looking at nothing, letting my thoughts drift, replaying the meeting. I sensed only a little unease among the board, but for the most part, the responses felt neutral. I wasn't home-free. I would still need to do more to repair the wedge.

IN ALL THE WORLD I HAVE ONLY FOUND ONE PERSON who truly understands me, who knows me completely: Ella Kate. In our adventurous life together we have lived many . . . I almost said many lives . . . but really, lived many places and been many things. Her support over the years has meant the world to me. I just want to make that clear. In everything I've done, in the churches I have led, in the troubles and successes that have been my life, she has been there beside me. I could not have done any of it without her help, and her love. But in the end, I'm the one responsible. I know that.

When the letters began to hound me, two churches before we came here, it was Ella Kate who urged me to fight the accusations, and later, to accept what we could not change, and move on. In the last church it was again Ella Kate who saw the end of the relationship before I did, who gave me the strength to just walk away, to find a new life and a new church here in Millville. It is something for which I will be grateful to the end.

HAVING PASSED THE TEST, SO TO SPEAK, I was anxious to get back to the work I felt called to do in Millville. There was the singular issue of rebuilding the congregation that I felt was paramount. With barely fifty members, the church would not survive any losses in membership. When Harold Humphries, the treasurer, proposed selling off fifty of the 65 acres the church owned, I could see that the board really wanted to be rid of the burden of funding the operation of the church. The acres, if they were sold, would bring in maybe $200-thousand. That could forestall the church's closing. It wouldn't prevent it, but it would reduce the need to think about it for maybe a decade more. And of course, that might be long enough for the church to regain sufficient members to carry on as before. A good plan, I agreed, but not the best one. A week later I had a plan on the table.

In my proposal the church would own and operate a small community for retirees. Not a nursing home, simply a community of small, one or two bedroom cottages built around the church and manse, to help some of the older congregants, and even non-members, move from empty nest to easy living. I had even gotten a local builder to design the houses and lay out the proposed plat for the community. Donald Tolliver had gone to the county zoning board to seek permission to build ten to twenty houses on the church property. We didn't know it at the time, but Gerald Lynn, a lawyer and retired county court judge, and a member of the church, had laid a similar proposal before the industrial development committee on an unspecified piece of property. That was about a month before the letters appeared.

ELLA KATE," I CALLED OUT, "WILL YOU SEE WHO'S AT THE DOOR?" Our doorbell almost never rang, especially because most people coming to the manse would just knock and walk in the back door, rather than the front. I was busy at my desk, making notes for my sermon for the coming Sabbath day. A lost traveler, perhaps, or maybe someone conducting a door-to-door mission. Ella Kate would handle it, I knew. The bell rang again, and I realized it was Tuesday, and Ella Kate was at the elementary school where she taught art. I got up and walked to the front door. A man in a suit was on the other side. Suits were odd in this community on a weekday morning; as odd as someone using the front door. I smiled as I turned the handle and pulled the door wide.

"Davis Lee Armstrong?" The man was tall, lean, hard looking. There was no smile on his face. I knew he was a policeman.

"Yes, I'm Davis Lee Armstrong."

"Charles Dickey, State Police Criminal Investigation." As he spoke he swung open his suit coat, reaching in to pull out a leather wallet with a badge and photo ID. The movement of the coat also revealed a shoulder holster and the butt of a business-like hand gun I recognized as a 9mm automatic.

"Come in, Mr. Dickey." I swung the door wider.

"Sergeant Dickey. And I'd rather you stepped outside, please." He turned as if to usher me past himself. I stood there for a moment.

"What's this about, Sergeant?"

"Just step outside, please, sir. I have everything I need to talk to you about in my vehicle." There was command in his voice, and I knew there was no point in arguing with him, so I stepped past him and we walked down the short sidewalk to his black, unmarked Chevrolet. At the car I turned to face him.

"Want to tell me what this is all about?"

"I want you to tell me about what's in these anonymous letters people in the community have been receiving." He opened the door of his car and reached in for a manila folder. Standing by the open door, his suit coat still unbuttoned and the left side caught on the shoulder holster (whether by accident or design I couldn't tell), he opened the folder. He held it close to himself, not letting me see what was in it, but instead, he read from what I knew was the letter that had been circulating for the last three months: "That Davis Lee Armstrong is not now, nor has he ever been, a minister, and that the academic degrees he claims to hold are total fabrications and lies." He closed the folder. "Strong stuff, Mr. Armstrong. Strong stuff."

"Why are you telling me this, Sergeant? I know what's in the letter, my congregation knows, and frankly, they have realized the false nature of the accusations and given me a vote of confidence."

131

"Is that so?" He threw the folder back into the car. "There seems to be some doubt about that, Mr. Armstrong," (I noted the emphasis on 'Mister') "and if the writer is accurate you are violating several laws in this state, including taking money under false pretenses, and even creating a scam to extract money from the church and its members."

"A scam? What are you talking about?" I tried to sound amused.

"This housing scheme you have proposed."

"Sergeant, there is nothing in that proposal that is false or illegal. I don't know what you or your superiors are up to, but my congregation has full confidence in me, or I wouldn't be here. As for the 'scheme' as you call it, there is nothing illegal about trying to use our resources for the betterment of the community." Before I could really get going, he grabbed the folder again, shaking it in my face.

"That letter's not all that we have, Armstrong. We'll get you, and expose you for what you are. Don't think we won't!" With that, he threw the folder back on the seat, slammed the door, walked around to the other side and got in. I stood there dumbfounded, as he started his car and drove away. I continued to stand there for at least a minute or more before turning and walking slowly back to the front door.

"Funny," I remember thinking. "I don't think I've ever used this door before."

GOLDIE NESBITT IS A GRANDMOTHERLY WOMAN, warm and forgiving by nature. The day after the policeman had come to the door, Goldie called the manse.

"Reverend, I want to let you know that I think the way some people are talking hereabouts is not the way all of us feel. You have real friends here, and not just among the church members."

"Mrs. Nesbitt, God bless you. I know that what you and the rest of the congregation are going through is unpleasant. Your words mean a lot to me and to Ella Kate, too."

"Not just words, Reverend. My nephew in Morsefield's a lawyer, and if you'll let him, I have told him he has to help you."

"Mrs. Nesbitt, that's so kind of you. Until yesterday I thought things were under control, but . . . well, they don't seem to be. Perhaps I do need to talk to your nephew."

"His name is Jordan. Robert Jordan. He's my brother's son. Wonderful boy, and I think you'll get on right well. He was going to be a preacher, too, but somewhere he got side-tracked into law. Still a spell-binder, I think. Just preaches in a different setting." She laughed, and I joined her. It was the first time I'd heard anything even a little humorous in days.

I took the phone number Goldie offered, writing it on the pad beside my computer, and hung up. Was I really going to use a lawyer this time? I'd had dealings with them in the other churches where this had happened, and my feeling was that they really didn't understand. Still, it might make a difference with the people here if they knew I had hired a lawyer.

Thinking back, one of the problems with these lawyers is that they want too much information that I'm not always prepared to give. I am who I am, and my work speaks for itself, I think. Still, if the state police were getting involved, I thought I'd better have someone else do the talking.

WHEN DONALD CALLED ME on Thursday morning, I had just sat down to look at the plans for the retirement community. Coincidentally he had just had a call from Gerald Lynn.

"Davis, I think something's going on here that you need to be aware of." Something more than was already happening? I thought I had fixed all of that. "Have you had much to do with Gerry Lynn?"

"No. He's always cordial, and seems to be interested in the church, but beyond seeing him on Sundays, I haven't had too much to do with him. Is he not well?" I always think that when there is a question like Donald's it will have to do with the well-being of one of my flock, but there is still room for a surprise or two in life.

"Oh, he's well enough, I suppose, but my question doesn't have anything to do with his health. In fact, it has more to do with yours. He wants the board to investigate you again."

"What's his position, Donald? He's not on the board."

"He offers legal advice to the church. Sometimes whether we ask for it or not."

"Oh. And has the board asked for it?"

"No. But that doesn't matter with him. Says he's been talking to the state police investigator."

"Maybe I should call on him, Donald. Go see him, maybe confront him to see if we can't stop him from making more out of this than there really is."

"I don't know. He can be pretty aggressive when it suits him."

"It may not show, my friend, but I can be, too. When I need to."

"I'll come with you if you want."

"I'd appreciate that, Donald. I really would."

WELL, NOW." THE ELDERLY MAN SAT BACK IN HIS SWIVEL CHAIR, a cigar clamped between his teeth, a non-committal smile on his face. He was a large man, though not very tall. I could see that when he leaned back his feet didn't quite touch the floor. "Well, now," he repeated. "What can I do for you two this mornin'?" His smile didn't change, his eyes, old and squinty and cold, focused on me. "You here 'bout this letter business, Reverend? 'Cause if you are, let me tell you that I have nothin' to do with the state police and their investigation." The smile left his face, he leaned forward, took the cigar out of his mouth and held it like a pointer, aimed at me. "But I'll tell you this: if you aren't what you say you are, I'll see you out of here on a rail, if I can. You understand that?" His chair creaked as he sat back, putting the cigar back between his stained teeth. "Now if there's nothing to it, of course, I'll be real happy for you. But for right now," he turned to Donald, "maybe you'd be smart to put that housing development on hold, don't you think?"

"Is that what you're after?" The idea flashed in my mind, and I said it before I could stop myself. "You want that land for yourself, don't you?"

"Careful, son," the old man hissed. "You don't want to start somethin' you cain't finish." When he wanted to make a point, The Judge lapsed into good-ole-boy speak.

We were both on our feet now. The Judge cleared his throat, as though he were calling two school boys to account. We stopped before we completely turned our backs on him.

"And Donald, I'd be real careful who I chose to support here, you know. Man does what this feller does, you might not want to be associated with him too close."

"Sorry, Judge," Donald turned quickly to face the fat old man, "did I misunderstand ? Has there been a trial we didn't know about? I thought a judge withheld judgment until all the facts had been examined."

I took Donald by the arm. "Come on," I said. "We'll see this through. Don't let it bother you. I'm used to it."

THE NEWSPAPER SEEMED TO BE HAVING A FIELD DAY with my story. A weekly, the "Millville Reporter" had taken up the "cause" with an editorial that reported ". . . a disconcerting rumor that a well-regarded minister in our community seems not to be what he claimed. In these times, when the leaders of so many of our national institutions appear to be apologizing for misrepresenting themselves to the public, it may seem perfectly normal, but to us, having someone in our midst who pretends to be not just a community leader, but a man of the cloth, would be an insult to the honesty and truth-telling we as a community demand of ourselves and our children."

Then the second letter arrived.

"Dear Reverend," the letter began, "I'm writing to warn you that there is an effort being made by some members of the church to bring formal charges against you here in . . ." The letter was not from anyone here in town. It was from the one real friend in the last church we had. The writer went on to say that some members of the church hierarchy had determined that I could be sued to force me to repay the salary and other benefits I had received from the church over the three years I was there. I hadn't expected that, not seen it coming at all. The writer went on to warn me that should I return to Oklahoma, I would probably be served with papers and so on. Well, I hadn't really planned to return to there anytime soon, so that wasn't a problem unless the state wanted to extradite me. It was just the idea, I guess, that left me shaken and uncertain. What would happen next? In a way this was all very exciting. It added a kind of urgent charge to my life. I was almost enjoying it. Almost, but not quite. In the first place I had never had to deal with law enforcement. In the past the people I had worked for had always felt that it was best if I moved on and nothing further was heard. That would mean less trauma for the community, and an easier transition for us. Now it seemed, I would have to not only hire a lawyer, but face the public humiliation of arrest and a trial in Millville. And of course, there was always the possibility of extradition to Oklahoma. If I lost in Millville, I was sure that would be next.

"ELLA KATE, WE SEEM TO BE IN A BIT OF TROUBLE." We were sitting at the kitchen table, where we spent much of our time when we were both at home. "I've been giving this whole business some serious thought. Maybe we should just close the door on this chapter." Ella Kate looked at me without speaking. I could see a great sadness coming into her eyes, a kind of melancholy resignation, I guess.

"Again, Lee?" Ella Kate was the only one who didn't call me "Davis" or "Davis Lee." (That was my mother's way when I'd done something wrong as a child.) "Where can we go this time?" She held her eyes locked on mine until I turned away.

"Maybe it's time to go back to Montana. Back home."

"There's not a church there that will want you, is there?" Her voice was tired and sad, and I felt a great weight in my own heart for the suffering I seemed to have imposed on this woman who had stood by me for so long.

"No, I guess I burned those bridges a long time ago. But your teaching license is still good there, isn't it?"

"Yes. And I guess the school here will give me a good

recommendation. They all seemed to like me." Ella Kate had always won the hearts of her students and the other teachers, regardless of what my own fortunes were. I was sure this time would be the same. At least I hoped it would be. I stood and walked around the table to stand behind her. Putting my hands on her shoulders I could feel the misery in them, and the tension, and then, just as quickly, those disappeared, to be replace by a resurgence of strength, strength I knew she would muster. I walked out of the kitchen and into my study, leaving the lights off, letting only the early moonlight guide me to my desk. I sat facing the dark bookshelves behind the desk, then swung round to look at the moonlit yard beyond the house. What was going wrong, I wondered? Why did this time seem different?

WHEN I WAS A BOY OF ABOUT TWELVE OR THIRTEEN, I realized I could sense what people wanted from me, and to provide it almost instantly. Most people are not aware that they divulge clues about themselves in the very first moments of contact. I'm very sensitive to that, and pick up on little things so that in a few minutes of conversation I can "connect," perhaps by identifying their place of birth or the college they went to, or the kind of work they do. I hear and retain little things, things people might not even remember saying, and work them back into the conversation. Without knowing why, people feel they have known me for a long time, and more importantly, that I know them. The bonding is almost instantaneous. I must admit that every time I work people this way it gives me something, a kind of thrill! It is so much a part of the way I work with people that it is as natural as shaking hands, yet it still speeds up my pulse when I sense it working. But now, I don't know, maybe it wasn't what I needed. Suddenly I was confronted with people who were very serious, who weren't about to bond. Perhaps I had miscalculated. That hadn't happened before.

IF YOU HAVE FOLLOWED THIS STORY FROM THE BEGINNING, or at

least from the time it first became public, then you know much of the rest of it. How the police came and arrested me, making sure they did it at the church when there were other people around. Why they couldn't wait until after the congregation had left, or until the next day, I didn't really understand at the time. I thought I detected a secret smile on Judge Lynn's face. He held it briefly, as I was approached by Sergeant Dickey in the fellowship hall.

"Mr. Davis Lee Armstrong, I have a warrant for your arrest." His voice was louder than I thought necessary, and his face showed just the trace of a smile as he held up a folded piece of paper. I couldn't sense any level of connection with the man. None. His professional face, I realized, was totally guarded by training and experience. "Come with me." He did have the grace to not whip out handcuffs, but that was about all.

Immediately members of my congregation surrounded us, and Donald Tolliver stepped quickly to my side.

"What's this," he said, reaching for the paper the policeman held. Dickey pulled the paper out of Donald's reach.

"You his lawyer?" The policeman was immediately defensive.

"Certainly not. I'm his friend."

"Then all you need to know is that this is a warrant for Mr. Armstrong's immediate arrest. I'm taking him into custody. If you're not his lawyer, I'd suggest you get in touch with whoever is." With that, the sergeant took me by the elbow and propelled, yes that's the word, propelled me out of the hall, and out to his black sedan. Still in sight of the congregation, he made a show of putting cuffs on me, then guiding my head as he steered me into the back seat. I was still too surprised, too shaken to offer any resistance, and I knew that it must have seemed an admission of guilt to those watching. But guilty of what? What had I really done? Had I hurt these people, or failed in anything I had promised them? As we drove away from the church I glanced back only once, to see the congregation standing in a random grouping around the front doors of the church. They weren't moving, but were simply staring after us. In the last flash of a frame I saw one short, heavy man step through the crowd, his cane sweeping the way ahead, until he stood in front of them all, the only animated figure I could see.

ELLA KATE AND DONALD WERE WAITING at the front desk of the regional prison when I came through the barred steel door from the cells. I had gone through the humiliation of being forced to empty my pockets, turn over my shoelaces and belt and had then been put in a holding cell with three others, men arrested for real crimes like being drunk in public, and skipping an alimony payment. Not how I should have liked to spend my Sunday, but still, I was able to give comfort to one or two of my cell-mates before I was called out.

"Donald has posted your bond," Ella Kate whispered as she hugged me, "and driven me over here to get you." She stood back and I turned to Donald

"Thank you my dear friend," I said, turning to take his hand. He looked me in the eye but said nothing, simply smiled a non-committal smile and stepped back. I turned to the desk officer and signed for my possessions, checking to be sure nothing had been lost, and then the three of us walked out into the evening. Donald and I sat up front, Ella Kate in the back, as we drove home. "Home" had a new meaning for me that night.

As we crossed the county we didn't speak. It was only when we were getting out of the car that Donald finally offered his thoughts.

"Davis, I'm not judging you or anyone else when I say this: there is something going on here that I can't decipher. It's not something I've had to deal with before. I will tell you this: if there is anything you can say or do that will clear this up, regardless of what it is, you need to do it. There's more here than just your job or your reputation. This church has weathered many storms, but it is particularly fragile right now, and too much is riding on what happens to you. And what happens to you, happens to all of us, regardless of what we think or believe." I wanted to interrupt, to reassure my friend, but I couldn't find the words. I simply smiled, stepped away from the car, and stood with Ella Kate as we watched Donald drive away. It was a sad, cold evening that welcomed us as we entered the house. I couldn't even face the blinking light on the answering machine. I closed the door to the study, and walked into the kitchen. Someone had been to the house and left a casserole on the stove, and put a pot of coffee on while we were away. Some in the congregation were answering, even without being asked. I was grateful.

WHEN THE WINTER WINDS BEGIN MOVING IN on this part of Montana, I know the end of the glorious Fall is upon us. When I sit up here, overlooking the little town in the valley, I can see the progress of the change moving down from the mountain. The colors progress from brilliant to faded, giving every day a new, less brilliant tint. It is a sad time for me now as it was when I was growing up here. But I'm glad to be back where I started.

The trial is over now, and the judgments rendered. That fine little church I grew to love is leaderless again, the congregation still reeling from the awful anger that spilled out at the hearings. I was surprised because I had never thought through what my effect on a community could be. I only knew that I wanted to bring good things to people, and show them that I could provide them with something no one else could. That had been my goal all along: to show everyone that just because I was a poor boy from an uneducated, back country family, I was full of ideas and creativity and ability. Nobody ever seemed to pay attention when I was just a school boy, except for my early preaching experiences here. Then they sat up and listened, I can tell you.

Having that much adulation poured over me when I took the pulpit as a boy preacher never was reproduced. Even with a title before my name, even with letters after it, I was only a preacher, only doing what was expected of me. Somehow, they never quite got it. Not here, not in Millville, not in Oklahoma or any of the other places I had been. Oh, I was liked well enough in most places, and even given extraordinary support when people received the letters calling me a fake, but no one ever said how smart I was, how brilliant I had been in their eyes.

The jury found me guilty of false pretenses, of stealing by accepting money for what I did (though I performed everything I had promised and then some), and of misleading and lying. Nobody ever said, in my defense, "Yes, but he was smart enough to fool us all." Nobody. That's what hurt the most. That's why I had to send them those letters. They were all so easily fooled. In the end, just as in those other places, I had to send those anonymous letters; had to accuse myself, so they could see how smart I was. How much smarter than the rest of them. Of all of you.

But it's over now. Something went very wrong there in Millville. Had that old judge not been so greedy, so full of his own plans for making money by buying the church's land at a bargain price, I think Millville would have ended just as the other places did: with Ella Kate and I slipping silently away, finding another place, laughing our private laugh as we drove out of town. But not this time. For one thing, I think Ella Kate finally tired of it all. Of the running away, the hiding, the shading of the truth.

IN A WAY, IT ALL BEGAN AS A JOKE. We met when she was a student, and I was working at the college as a janitor. I'd often find her in the art department after hours, working on a drawing or a painting, and we'd chat as I cleaned up around her. One night I found a couple of diplomas in the trash, and pulled them out. "Do you make these here?" I had never thought about where such things came from.

"We do the lettering, when they ask us to. Those were some that had misspelled names or words, I guess."

"Seems wasteful to throw them away. Could they be erased?"

"I guess so. Let me see." She took one and using an electric eraser, deleted the misspelled word, then with a pen she re-lettered the space. I couldn't see any difference.

"You could save the school some money if you corrected the mistakes. Maybe they'd give you an extra grade." Ella Kate laughed and said she'd show it to her professor the next day.

When I came to the studio the next night, Ella Kate was there again. As I walked in, she looked up, smiled, and said, "I have something for you." I walked over to her table and she handed me a neatly lettered diploma with my name on it. "My professor said I shouldn't bother trying to save the forms, but he admired my initiative. I think I'll get an A for this semester." And we laughed. And I've kept that diploma all these years. I guess that was the beginning of a lot of things.

It's been almost forty years. She's been a good companion and champion, but I think it finally caught up with her. She just didn't want to do it anymore. Millville was the only place where she ever said she wanted to stay. She told me that on the long drive home, to these mountains. Perhaps I misjudged her understanding of me, and her appreciation of my abilities. I don't know. I hope not. Still, this is the last place, the refuge we have, and it is the only place I could bring her to stay.

Ella Kate is still now, lying beside me on the soft bed of leaves. The warmth is leaving her body even as I dictate this last tape, even as I prepare the final step in the journey we have taken together. I will leave the tape running. The last sound, the discharge of the second bullet, will serve as a final period to the life and love I have experienced, regardless of the pain. But the worst part is that nobody ever recognized how smart I had to be to do it at all.

THE REPORT OF A SMALL CALIBER GUN is followed after several seconds, by the colorful song of a bird.

Treasure!

"All that glisters is not gold," Shakespeare wrote. Sometimes treasure that is buried is best left where you find it. Otherwise you risk losing a treasure you already possess.

DANCING WAS SARAH BROWn's LIFE until she discovered photography. Photography was her life until she discovered Edgar McCleod. Her understanding of the dancer's art, of the way the body moved and how sets, costumes and lights affected the image, gave her photographs a special intimacy and perspective. She left the Corps de Ballet to younger performers, but she never lost her dancer's body.

She discovered that dance imitated the shapes and movements of the natural world, and her work began to appear in magazines and journals devoted to nature an to art. Where once she traveled as part of an ensemble, she now ventured alone. From stage to city park, from parkland to country, from America to lands far away. The turns of her career moved in widening circles as white swans would encircle a queen on the edge of a lake. From new York to Nepal, her camera carried her as surely as strong arms had lifted her from the stage. It was a good life. It had its dangers and rewards as any life fully lived should; challenging and satisfying.

EDGAR MCCLEOD LEARNED WOODCRAFT and the secrets of hunting and fishing from his father and grandfather. By the time he was in college he was a regular contributor to outdoor magazines, writing about outdoor gear. With a degree in mechanical engineering, he progressed to stories about science, technology and invention. His articles were in demand, and he had published several well-received general reader books on those subjects. His vigorous outdoor life and his writing life were completely integrated. What he did wasn' t for everyone, but it suited him perfectly. Tall, skin tanned and weathered by frequent hunting and fishing expeditions, Edgar looked and moved like a much younger man. If it was sometimes lonely he was also someone who relished solitude and the challenge of depending entirely on himself. Sarah was the only one he admitted to his private universe.

EDGAR AWOKE EARLY, AT FIRST LIGHT. He had come to this rocky campsite in the fading light of afternoon, made his camp, and when the sky was bright with stars fell asleep easily and slept well. He was fully packed up when Sarah arrived about nine. Had he not been facing the trail, he would not have heard her. Moving easily, effortlessly among the rocks, her breathing slow, she presented a picture of a healthy woman, dressed appropriately in hiking boots, cargo shorts, a loose, long-sleeved shirt and a wide-brimmed felt hat.

"You must be Sarah Brown," Edgar said, standing and walking to meet her. "Good morning." Sarah took the offered hand, shook it firmly and smiled up at him. She immediately felt comfortable in the presence of the tall, tanned, bearded man.

"You look just like your picture," she aid. "I hope I haven't kept you waiting."

"I've been here since last night, but no, you haven't,"

"You camped here?" It wasn't very welcoming: a bare rock outcrop, the only trees those that grew below the top of the ridge, and no water.

"I did. Not a bad place, really. Lots of sky to cover me," Though they had never met, each knew the other by reputation and work. Oddly, Sarah realized later, there was none of that wariness two creative people might naturally have, meeting for the first time; two who had sought solitude and privacy beyond all else.

The small talk accompanied them as Sarah took off her backpack and began to unload cameras, a tripod, folding reflectors and kits of filers and lenses.

From his own packs Edgar brought out the small and large camping tools that would be featured in the article and placed them on his sleeping bag. The first thing he realized about Sarah even before he was aware of her attractiveness, was the competence she exhibited in selecting her equipment and setting up the shots. Her direction was sure and simple: a move, a posture, a grip and when he had things set up the way she wanted them, the pictures were quickly made.

The images Sarah captured required less and less direction from either of them as the morning ran on. Instead they focused on each other, discovered mutual friends, places and experiences they had shared without being together, and that they had similar needs and expectations.

Nether had ever married or sought long-term relationships but suddenly, in a single day working together, they knew that "we have arrived at the same place at the same time, with the same needs and desires and feel as if we have suddenly been placed on a new earth for a new life." That was in the first of many love letters Edgar would compose for Sarah. She said it was the first treasure she had ever had.

INTIMACY, HARD FOR BOTH OF THEM, was slowly acquired over a courtship that spanned nearly two years. At first Sarah resisted Edgar's invitations to spend more than a day in the wilderness, though it was obvious to him that she was no stranger to nature's great places. As often as possible they worked together. Too often they were apart because their work demanded it. When they could manage a day or two it was just a weekend at a cabin on some remote mountainside, and they slowly, carefully, peeled way their layers of experience to find their shared needs, much as, after their third meeting, they had peeled away the clothes that barred intimacy.

When Edgar finally asked Sarah to marry him, it came as no surprise, but rather as the most natural direction their separate lives could take. It happened when they had been camping for a week on a secluded lake in Maine' s Arootook County near the Canadian border. As they drifted slowly along the shore in Edgar's canoe, Sarah began to talk about another experience on another lake.

"There is something I want to tell you before I say 'yes,' Edgar. It has to do with something that happened a long time ago, something very personal."

"A 'true confession,' Sarah?"

"Yes." She paused, letting her hand slip into the water, letting the water slide between her long fingers. "Yes, a confession of sorts but an explanation too." She lifted her hand from the water, watched the droplets slide from her fingertips back onto the moving surface, make a little dimple and then disappear.

"It's about why I was reluctant to come camping with you at first." She took a deep breath as if readying herself for a climb. "I love being in the woods, being at one with the earth and the trees and as much as possible, with the animals. They don't frighten me, not at all. I've been close to them, close enough to know them by their scent, some of them; by the sounds they make going through the brush even. I would not want to give it up, but once I almost did.

"A bad experience?"

"One I find it hard to talk about even today."

"It isn't something you have to do Sarah. Not for me . . . for you, maybe for us; not for me."

"I guess It's not so much what happened, but what could have happened, and what it was like, knowing."

"Knowing?"

"Living with an interrupted story, I guess. Something that might have happened but didn't, and yet it filled my dreams and idle thought for a long time"

"If it's too painful . . . "

"But I want you to know. I think if we are going to continue . . . well, continue as we are . . . to be together forever . . . then you need to know."

"When you're ready."

"Do you remember me telling you that I had started to hike the Appalachian Trail but never finished it?"

"Yes. A lot of people do that. Start and don't finish. I've been on parts of it but doing the whole route seems an end in itself; a medal to win."

"Exactly. Something people do to be able to say they have done it. Anyway, I'd left the main trail late one afternoon, uncomfortable with the number of others hiking that week. For three nights, when I'd arrive at one of the shelters along the trail, it would be crowded, overrun by couples and groups and one night a whole family out for a short overnight. It was fine as long as there was room to camp nearby, but I have always looked to the woods for solitude. I guess I should have known better than to try the trial at that time of year. Still, I was headed south hoping to get to Virginia or somewhere near it before the end of September. So that night I slipped off the trail, found a cozy little glen by some water, and settled in. I hadn't put up my tent, or even opened my backpack. I was hot and in need of a good scrubbing, frankly. The water was a clear little pond, so I decided to get clean before I did anything, and before it got full dark.

"What happened next was terrifying and stupid. As I came out of the water a man appeared in front of me. I backed away into the water again, and he laughed and picked up my underwear. Just then there was a rustling and movement behind him. I looked up, afraid it would be another man, but it was a bear! The man took off running. The bear moved after him, ignoring me. I slipped out of the water, hearing lot of thrashing about in the woods. I grabbed what I could from the ground and then climbed as high as possible in a huge pine tree. I hugged the tree for a while, covered myself with what I had grabbed, and remained in the tree all night. The bear never came back, but other animals came to the water. One, it may have been a coyote or a stray dog, sniffed at my pack but didn't come to the tree. Maybe it was that the water had washed me clean of scent, or that the breeze was coming off the water toward me. As the sky brightened I slipped out of the tree, dressed and got back on the trail and off to civilization." Sarah paused, letting the emotion of reliving that moment, that time, hang in the air between them.

"Before I left the trail again, I met other hikers who had already heard stories of a man mauled by a bear. The enormity of my situation, of what had almost happened, wouldn't have stopped me, I don't think, if I hadn't made another terrible error in judgment."

"You told someone about what happened?"

"I went to the police. The local papers were wondering what the man was doing in the woods, and then someone . . . it may have been the investigator . . . let it be known that the man had a 'feminine undergarment' in his hand when they found him. They were searching the area for another victim. They had teams of searchers in the woods, and I thought it was my duty to tell them what happened."

"A circus?"

"Oh, yes," she said quietly. "And it was humiliating and frightening and just the worst thing that had ever happened to me." Sarah paused. Edgar bent forward from his seat in the stern of the canoe. Taking Sarah's hands in his, he pulled her close, felt the tension draining.

Taking a deep breath, as if to gird herself, she continued: "I was besieged, chased, identified and even speculated about: my relationship with the dead man, and why we were in the woods in the first place. The fact that the dead man had a police record, was a known sex offender, carried little weight with the press or the public."

"I don't read the papers much, but I seem to remember hearing about that. In fact I still remember a headline I saw in some paper, probably in the checkout line in a grocery store: *"WILDLIFE FOTOG FINDS LIFE IN THE RAW!"*

Sarah tensed again at the memory, then went on. "I made another mistake, too. I called a friend . . . you don't know him . . . and asked him to please come and get me. I didn't know what else to do. I had called him before I talked to anybody. When he showed up the press was in full cry, and unbelievably, he couldn't understand why I was so upset. I think, at some level, he even half-suspected that I was partially responsible for the whole incident. Oh, Edgar! I couldn't believe what was happening to me. I just wanted to crawl away and hide. In the end, I didn't have to. Howard was out of my life and I was so alone . . . and that's the way I stayed until I met you."

"I can only imagine what it must have been like for you, Sarah, but it won' t ever happen again as long as I' m alive. Believe me darling, I' m your protector and lover and everything else you need me to be."

NOW IN THEIR EARLY FIFTIES, they had been married for ten years. When they were not traveling on assignment or doing research away from home, they lived on 160 acres of remote mountain farmland. The woods and fields provided both with an ever-changing, always challenging and inspiring natural studio.

THE CHAIN SAW POPPED AND STOPPED, out of gas. Edgar put it down on the stump of the tree he had just cut. While the saw cooled he took out the tools he would need to sharpen and tighten the chain. He drove a portable bar clamp into the stump, secured the bar and got to work. Rolling the chain a few inches at a time, he lightly touched up the teeth with a thin, round file. Satisfied with the sharpness of the chain, he refilled the tank, then the oil reservoir, wiped up the few spilled drops, then reached for the bright metal gas can cap. It wasn't there, and not anywhere on the makeshift work surface of the stump. He searched among the leaves and other detritus around the stump but couldn't find it. "Damn!" He looked up, saw he still had a few hours of light, and headed for the house, on the other side of the hill.

In his workshop, Edgar rooted around in the parts bins but couldn't find a spare cap. Giving up, he opened a closet and pulled out a simple metal detector. He walked back up the hill to the tree stump.

At first the detector had little to say to him. A silence in fact, was all it produced once it was adjusted. Sweeping it over the ground around the stump, he finally heard the high-pitched whine that indicated metal under the duff. Stooping, he ran his hand under some leaves, and found the small metal cap. Standing up and turning, the detector began to whine again. "Well, well. What else have I lost here?" He took a step forward. The whine grew in intensity. Swinging the detector in an arc, the noise diminished, then increased again as he swung back.

"Now what in the word could make a noise that big?" He used his boot to clear the area. "Probably some old car parts," he mused. The farmers who had owned the land for a hundred years buried cans and broken tools and other junk around the house and barn, and in remote places among the trees. Still, it was intriguing.

By the time he had finished cutting up the tree and stacking the logs, it was getting dark. Edgar packed up and returned to the shop. Putting tools away and cleaning up took half-an-hour. While his hands did the work his mind focused on what might be hidden in the ground.

Sitting at the table an hour later, Edgar told Sarah about the metal detector's unfinished story.

"What do you think it is?"

"Well, I've already found half a pick-up truck, two wagon wheels, and lots of other big pieces of equipment sticking out of the ground here and there, but I don't know. Could be anything."

"Going to dig it up?"

"Maybe. Depends on the weather. I want to take the tractor and wagon up there tomorrow and bring the wood down, so I'll take a few tools up and scratch around a little."

"Sounds like fun. I'll come up with you and take pictures. Maybe there's a story in it." Sarah liked being in the woods with her husband, and taking pictures of him at work added to the pleasure.

Edgar almost always spent mornings working on whatever freelance article he had on his desk or dealing with the editors who made their semi-retirement possible. Sarah followed a similar schedule, either outdoors or in her studio. It was after lunch, about two in the afternoon, that the couple arrived at the pile of logs Edgar had cut the day before. Using the detector again, he located the place where the sound was most intense.

"It couldn't be too big, could it?" Sarah knew the soil here was only inches deep with a thick layer of rock not far below the surface. She had gardened enough in the last few years to understand why the previous owners had finally given up farming. But the land was perfect for what she and Edgar wanted: privacy, isolation from urban life, the serenity of trees and fields and wildlife.

Together they loosened and shoveled the thin soil. It seemed deeper here, and in fact if they moved too far in any direction, the pick or hovel would clang against rock and send a vibration up the wooden handle. But where they dug easily, a rectangular pattern began to emerge. It was about one-and-a-half by two feet, and seemed to offer no resistance through a foot of hard-packed soil. Sarah, helping to remove the loose earth, occasionally stopped, picked up one of her cameras, and added to the documentation of the digging. Now, in the middle of the rectangle, the sound changed. A flat, resonant metallic sound returned from the light tap Edgar made with his pick. He stopped. Sarah picked up her camera to capture the quizzical look on his face.

Putting aside the tools, the two worked with their hands to clear away the last few inches of soil. A wide, long piece of bright metal the size of the excavation reflected the blue sky. Wide metal bands crossed the narrow width of the surface. A thick, steel D-shaped ring was secured midway in each band.

"What do you think it is?"   Sarah' s breathing was quick.

"Could be anything. Maybe a coffin, or it could be buried treasure," Edgar betrayed no sign of excitement,   "Of course," he added as a hedge,   "it could also be the top of a feed box that wasn't any good and they just dropped it on the ground one day. Like a lot of the stuff I've found here. But the ground around it has been cut down into the rock, and you don't do that for an old box lid."

Edgar and Sarah used a digging bar and a shovel to clear around the edges of the hole. Sticking his fingers into the opening they made, Edgar could feel metal below that.

"Stainless steel," he announced, scratching the surface. "Must have been formed in a single piece."

"Are we going to try to get it out?" Sarah looked at the sky, the winter light fading quickly. They had been at the hole far longer than she had realized. As excited as they both were, she was tired, and thought Edgar must be too.

"It's going to take a bit to get it up," he said. "Let's load the logs and tools and come back tomorrow when we're fresh."

"Let's leave the logs, too." Sarah realized she hadn't the energy to help. "It'll be too dark by the time we get the wagon loaded."

Edgar looked at his wife, seeing the tiredness, felt his own, and agreed. Leaving the wagon and the tractor, the couple walked silently hand-in-hand down the hill to the cozy log house. Coals from the morning fire were still glowing in the stove. Edgar rearranged the embers and added a couple of pieces of wood. The flames came up quickly as he closed the iron door.

Dinner that night was a thick venison stew Sarah had put on the stove in that morning. As they ate they speculated about the mysterious find. "Could be a box of loot from the Civil War," Sarah offered. "I know there were some soldiers moving through here at one time."

"I think the soldiers were further back up the valley. Aren't there some caves up there?"

Sarah nodded. "Up by Beulah's home place." Edgar always smiled when city-girl Sarah lapsed into the local vernacular. Sarah had made friends with their neighbor up the valley and sometimes walked the half-mile dirt road to spend an afternoon with her. The old woman was pleased to have someone who listened to her stories. "Or it could have been someone who lived up that hollow trying to protect their valuables from the looters." Cleary, Sarah had decided there was something valuable beneath the metal

155

top.

"Of course," Edgar returned to his first guess of the day before, "it's more likely to be just a box of junk. A lot of stuff that accumulated with nowhere to put it. Tin cans, broken tools, that kind of thing. Anyway, the steel is modern, not Civil War."

"Oh, come on Ed. Let's pretend a little." Sarah laughed and got up, stepped closer to her husband and kissed him gently on the cheek. "Maybe it will just be junk, but wouldn't it be neat to find a real treasure?" Edgar put his arms around her and pulled her onto his lap.

"City Sarah, my girl, I found my treasure long ago. But we can dream anything you want. We're not too old to dream."

IN THE MORNING, A LITTLE EARLIER THAN USUAL, Edgar was ready to leave the house. Sarah, who tended to be a late riser, came into the kitchen dressed and ready to go before Edgar finished his first cup of coffee.

"Fancy a walk in the woods?"

Edgar stood up and gave Sarah a hug and a kiss. "Better have something to eat before we go. Could be a long day."

"I've eaten and packed a lunch." Sarah pointed to the small cooler on the countertop. "Ready when you are." She pulled her down jacket from the peg by the door and slipped it on. Slender as she was, the puffy blue jacket gave her a roly-poly look that always brought a smile to Edgar's face. His own clothing tended to be lighter: jeans, a sleeveless down vest over a long-sleeved heavy wool shirt and thermal undershirt. In their boots, hats and gloves the couple looked ready for the wilderness. Picking up the cooler Edgar opened the door for Sarah and they walked up the hill again.

Standing on either side of the opening, they looked at the metal slab without speaking. From the wagon Edgar lifted a four-foot steel chain, knelt and ran the links through the rings on the box.

"They still look sturdy. Guess we'll test 'em first, though." Leaving the chain on the lid, Edgar returned to the tractor, started it, backed it around and moved it so that the bucket loader on the front was over the lid. Lowering it, he stopped just above the chain. Turning the engine off, he stepped to the ground and, with Sarah's help, hooked the ends of the chain to the outer-most teeth of the bucket.

"If this holds, we'll have whatever this is above ground in no time. But I wouldn't count on it."

He walked back to the tractor, climbed up and started the engine. As the bucket began to rise, the chain links clanked and pulled taut. Using the hydraulic power of the tractor, Edgar exerted a steady pull, afraid to jerk it upward because he wasn't sure the bands and rings would take the strain. He kept the pressure on, then relaxed it, returned the pressure again, the let it off, and each time it seemed the buried object moved a little. The fourth time he let the bucket down there was a noticeable movement in the hole. It took almost fifteen minutes of pulling and easing before the earth released its hold on what it had so long protected. Still moving the bucket slowly, Edgar eased it up, up until the metal was clear of the ground. Without stopping he raised what now was recognizable as a box about eighteen inches wide, two feet long and a foot thick. Slowly he began backing the tractor in a tight arc. When the box was over the farm wagon he carefully lowered it to the bed. He eased the bucket down a little more until there was slack in the chain. Sarah hoisted herself up onto the bed and pulled the chain off the bucket teeth. The links coiled on top of the box with a solid "thunk."

Backing away, Edgar lowered the bucket, turned off the engine and stepped down to the ground. He joined Sarah at the back of the wagon and they stood silently looking at what they had retrieved. On the wagon it looked small. The bands were pitted but intact, and seemed to be single pieces. Carefully Edgar ran his hands over the metal.

"Whoever built this didn't intend it to be opened and closed a lot." He tapped the rivets that secured the bands, "A drill will take those out pretty quickly."

Sarah looked at her husband and smiled. She loved to watch him when he was solving a problem: the concentration on his face, brow slightly furrowed, one hand stroking his chin, the other supporting the elbow. She placed her hand on his arm and moved closer.

"Are we going to load the wood before we go?" Her question was asked with a lightness that belied her own anticipation.

Edgar looked down at his wife's upturned face and kissed her lightly. "Let's think about this a bit." Reaching for the cooler they had brought, he walked over to the tree stump and sat down. "Time for lunch anyway."

"Ed!" She almost made in into two syllables. "How can you be hungry now?" Curiosity was overriding her customary caution.

"Sarah, it may be nothing more than a box of bricks, you know. Or a coffin. Or just what it looks like: a steel tractor weight. If it's a coffin, then we really shouldn't even have taken it out of the ground. Maybe I need to do a little research before we try to open it."

"Research? Edgar, what are you going to do, Google steel box or steel coffin? Come on, love, let's find out what we have."

"We have," Edgar said, looking into the cooler, "what appear to be chicken sandwiches, two apples, potato chips, and a thermos of coffee." He smiled up at his wife. "Come, sit and we'll decide while we eat."

Reluctantly, Sarah found room on the stump beside her husband, and accepted the sandwich he dug out of the cooler. She was hungry, but really! There was so much more of interest. Still, she unwrapped the sandwich and began to eat. Both ate silently, never looking at anything except the box.

Now that it was out of the ground and resting at eye level, they could see that it was indeed a smooth box with a well-fitted top. The edges of the lid extended about three inches below the top.

"It's certainly a box. Well-made, too. Just look at the welds on the top and bottom and at the corners."

"How long do you think it's been there?"

"Hmm. Not too long. Even stainless steel will eventually corrode in the ground. Maybe ten years. We know the Sherman family settled here a hundred years ago, and I'd think that if this was a family treasure they would have looked for it before they let the property go. Unless, of course, they didn't know it was here." He paused. "Or it's just a box of tin cans."

Sarah took the apple she was holding and pushed it into Edgar's mouth. "Stop that! I want to hear about buried treasure, not tin cans."

Edgar removed the apple and gave Sarah a very wet, apple-tart kiss. "Okay, but just keep that in the back of your mind."

While Edgar picked up tools and put them on the wagon, Sarah used the excellent light to photograph the box from all sides. When they had both finished, she vaulted herself onto the wagon, Edgar mounted the tractor and set the speed for a slow trip down the hillside. He pulled the tractor and trailer into the metal barn, stopping just under a chain hoist that hung from the ceiling. Locking the brakes, he climbed down and walked to the back of the wagon. Sarah jumped lightly into his arms and they turned and looked again at the box. At that moment the phone in the barn rang. Edgar walked over and answered it. While he talked, Sarah studied the box. It didn't look very old after all in the bright light of the barn.

"Have to go to the house for a few minutes," Edgar said. "Jennifer Bowles needs me to read a change they want to make. They're ready to lock up the story and need my okay. I want to see it first." He walked out the door, across the courtyard and into the house.

Sarah began to take more pictures with a medium focus lens. As she framed a shot, with the doorway in the background, a man suddenly appeared in the viewfinder: a narrow face, small chin, pale white skin. His hair was lank, dirty blonde, combed straight back revealing a receding hairline. The electronic camera noiselessly captured the image. Holding the camera as if she were still about to take the picture, she looked up at the stranger.

"Can I help you?"

The man let a quick unexpressive smile, not more than a twitch of his lips, cross his face as he stepped into the well-lit shop area.

"I was hoping to get permission to hunt here. Used to back when I was a boy." The accent, Sarah noted, wasn't quite local. "You a Sherman?"

Laughing, Sarah explained that they had bought the Sherman property several years ago.

"You must not have been here in a while."

"No. been out west. Just back for a visit."

"Are you related to the Sherman family?" Her photographer's eye had quickly seen the resemblance in his face.

"Oh, distant you might say." He walked further into the barn. Dressed in faded camouflage shirt and trousers, he wore boots that were much newer looking. His shoulders supported a backpack that hung limply, as if it were empty. Attached to one side was a small folding shovel. He held a worn-looking rifle equipped with a scope. On his head he wore a camouflage cap that looked as new as his boots. He pointed to the box.

"What you got there?"

"Oh, we don't know. My husband found it in the woods."

"Looks like its been in the ground awhile."

"Edgar says it could be old, but we don't know. It's heavy though."

"Want some help opening it? I'm pretty good with my hands." The man put his hand out and touched the cold metal tentatively, almost caressingly. His hands, Sarah noticed, were pale, smooth, not used to hard work.

Edgar came across the gravel to the barn. Without quite knowing why, Sarah felt relieved to have him back in the building. She turned to her him.

"This is Mr. –," She turned to the man, "I'm sorry, I didn't ask your name?"

"Dickie," he said, and nothing more.

"Yes, this is Dickie." She turned to him again: "Dickie or Mr. Dickie?"

"Just Dickie."

"Doing a little hunting?" Edgar studied the figure before him.

"Hoping to. I was telling your missus I used to hunt here a long time ago. Didn't know the Shermans were gone."

"What are you looking for?" Edgar studied Dickie's gun.

"Bear season. Thought I'd get me a bear. You hunt?"

"A little. Looks like you've had that rifle a long time." Edgar pointed to the Marllin 30-06 the man held. "You like that for bear?"

"It'll do."

In his mind, Edgar compared the gun with the heavier lever-action Winchester 88 and nearly obsolete .358 Winchester shells he had used for years. The two men looked at each other. Sarah could sense information passing between them.

"We need to lock up now, and go back to the house." Turning to Dickie, he nodded toward the door and said, "Sorry about the hunting. We don't open the woods to anyone anymore, it would keep us too confined to the house."

Dickie, holding the gun by the forestock, raised it in salute and turned to leave.

"Well, I'll be camping nearby for the next couple of days. I'll check back in case you change your mind." He walked slowly to the door.

"No chance of that. Besides, I've seen no sign of bear this season, except beyond us on the state preserve. You'd probably do pretty well over there. Not many people in the woods yet."

The man waved over his shoulder and headed down the driveway. Edgar locked the door and the couple crossed the ten or so yards of gravel to the house.

"He didn't seem too put out," Sarah commented as they walked.

"He didn't seem too much of a hunter, either."

In the house, Sarah poured a cup of tea for herself and a cup of coffee for Edgar.

"I'm going to download the pictures and feed them to the big screen," indicating the flat-screen TV on the wall. "Maybe see something we haven't noticed."

The weekly paper had arrived in the mail, and Edgar looked through it as he drank his coffee. Sarah went into her studio and connected the camera to the computer. In a few minutes the images were ready to display on the big screen.

The pictures came up, responding to a remote control Sarah held in her hand. Edgar let the paper fall back on the table. In sequence, Sarah's pictures related the story of the digging and retrieval, the loading and transport of the mystery box now resting on the wagon. In the last frame, Dickie's face was visible.

"How'd you get that shot?"

"He was standing by the doorway when I took it."

"Can you zoom in on him?"

Sarah manipulated the remote and the screen was filled with Dickie's face.

"He sure looks like a Sherman," she said.

Edgar stood up, letting the paper fall back on the table. Had he looked at the bottom of page one, he would have seen Dickie's face again, although not nearly so well portrayed. FBI mug shots seldom enhance the subject. The article told of armed robbery, murder, unrecovered loot, escape after years in a mid-western prison; a story with a local slant.

THE DANCERS SEEMED TO FLY across the forest setting, landing softly and perfectly balanced. Bejeweled tiaras flashed in counterpoint to diamond-studded swords as the men and weightless women danced among the sweeping boughs of the woodland. A shuffling noise penetrated Sarah's dream; slipped into the ballet. The music faded as she opened her eyes. A light was falling through the open doorway of the bedroom. Turning over, she reached out for Edgar.

"You there?" she muttered sleepily. He was not. Slowly, Sarah peeled back the covers and sat up. "Edgar?" she said more loudly. "You having trouble sleeping?"

She got out of bed and walked into the living room. "Can I make you" . . . it was not Edgar. Instead, just by the front door, his hand running over the key rack, stood Dickie.

"What – where's Edgar?" Her voice was higher pitched, a combination of stress and fear.

"He's outside, where he'll stay." His voice was tense and gravelly. He advanced quickly to Sarah. At once she was aware of her near nakedness. The long cotton nightshirt could hardly hide her from this man's eyes. She stepped back but he was faster. Grabbing her wrist, he spun her around and pushed her toward the open door. "We're going out, too."

He jangled the key to the barn in front of her face. He pushed her through the open door and out onto the cold gravel. The stones pricked her bare feet, but she hardly felt them as Dickie propelled her along.

Trying to twist out of the man's grip, she saw her husband lying face-down on the driveway. He wasn't moving.

"Stop! Stop!" she cried. "Why is Edgar on the ground?"

Dickie increased the pressure on the woman's arm and forced her to the barn's side door. As she struggled against him he held her tight to his chest, and as the door swung open he dropped the key and let his free hand slide over the tense body beneath the cotton.

"No! Stop it! Don't!" The words only brought a low laugh from Dickie, a laugh she felt through his chest pressed against her back.

Flipping the light switch by the door, he forced her forward to the end of the wagon and pushed her face-down onto the bed beside the box.

"Now the only thing I have to decide is what to open first." His voice was low and breathless. Releasing Sarah's wrist, he grabbed her nightshirt and rolled her over, at the same time pulling the thin material up. He began pulling at his own clothes. Sarah cried out her husband's name. The man simply laughed.

"No one to help lady. Just me."

Sarah screamed again. Pulling her knees up to her chest, she suddenly launched herself with all the muscle and strength her years of dancing had given her. Both feet smashed hard against Dickie's chest, knocking the breath out of him, and driving him backward. He stumbled and twisted, trying to regain his balance. He was just in time to see Edgar coming through the door.

His head bloody, dirt from the driveway on his face, Edgar grabbed a pick leaning against the wall by the door and staggered forward. Raising the steel tool above his head, he brought the twelve-inch point down hard. The steel went through the ribs, through the heart and out, below the shoulder blades. Edgar had placed the point as accurately as if he were shooting an arrow into a raging bear. Without stopping he twisted the handle, pulled the man to the side, and let him fall to the floor. The exposed tip of the steel made a "chink" sound as it touched the hard surface. Dickie rolled over on his side, twitched, offered one agonal, final breath, and lay still.

Another step brought Edgar to Sarah. Fear and adrenalin had left her shaking and cold. Taking her in his arms, he lifted her from the wagon. Gaining strength with every step, he carried her back to the house.

Gently Edgar lowered his wife to the bed. Wrapping her in the warm down comforter, he held her tightly in his arms.

"Oh, Edgar. Make love to me, now. Make his face go away." Sarah kept her eyes open, focused on Edgar's face, erasing for all time the image of Dickie Sherman. They slept.

AT FIRST LIGHT EDGAR SLIPPED OUT OF THE WARM AND LOVING ARMS that wrapped around him. He had a job to do. Washing the dried blood from his hair and face, he dressed, put on his boots and vest, grabbed a loose wool hat from the rack, and walked to the barn.

With one foot he held the cold body against the floor and pulled the pick from the dead man' s chest. The overhead chain hoist he had planned to use to take the box from the wagon he used instead to lift the body onto the bed.

The barn door swung open and with the tractor in low gear Edgar McCleod drove back to the place in the woods. It took an hour with the bucket on the tractor to enlarge the hole. Strapping the body to the bucket, he lifted it and moved it over the hole, then lowered it without ceremony into the three foot by six foot opening. With the heavy chain again hooked to the steel box, he picked it up, swung around and lowered it into the ground, letting it rest on the man who had put it there in the first place. Another hour saw the earth restored, leaves and branches scattered to cover the scar. Dickie was reunited with his treasure.

Edgar headed home to his.

A Hole In The Ground

A small town in Virginia's Shenandoah Valley is hardly the place a terrorist cell would hide. For someone with a past, like Lissa King, it might seem just the place to go and forget. Or be forgotten.

THE TOWN OF BEVERLEY LIES IN VIRGINIA'S UPPER SHENANDOAH VALLEY; "upper" because of elevation. Set between the Blue Ridge on the east and the Appalachians on the west, it has long been a center of economic life in the region. Like Virginians themselves, the town holds onto its place in history, and over the years has preserved the buildings and even the brick sidewalks and early lamp posts from the time before "modernization" swept so many small American towns away. Unlike those left in the dust of urban renewal, Beverley retained its charm and small-town atmosphere of long-ago. Chief among its attractions is Romany Hill Park, named for the seasonal visitors who stopped there in years gone by. There is almost always someone taking advantage of the walks and roads and park amenities. On a day in Spring, even at first light, there will be people there.

BLONDE HAIR, SHORT AND LOOSE, BOUNCES JOYFULLY in the slanting early morning light. It adorns the head of a tall, fit young woman, running freely along the otherwise empty roadway that circles the public park. In another fifteen minutes or so the other runners and early morning dog walkers will be along, but right now she's running alone. Now she slows and finally begins to walk. Her senses, always alert, set off an alarm. There is something unusual just to her right. There, in the bushes, not three feet from a large metal trash barrel, is a bag. No, three bags. Neatly stacked, obviously not just thrown at the trash can, but deliberately placed where they are. The runner stops before the stacked bags. She uses the toe of one running shoe to touch the top bag. What is she expecting? Will the plastic, pulled tighter, reveal the outline of a head, or an arm? What a thing to think! *But that's the way my mind works,* she tells herself.

The thin plastic, pulled tight and better illuminated by the horizontal rays of the rising sun, shows a shape resembling a brick, but something even more interesting: money -- stacks of bills! She steps away, walks a few feet, reaches inside her jacket pocket and pulls out her cell phone. As she presses the keys she turns in a circle, searching the shadows for someone who might be watching her.

"Police Department, Good morning, How may I direct your call?"

"I need to talk to an officer."

"Do you know the name of the officer you are calling?"

"No, I don't. Is there anyone in Investigations at this hour?"

"No, ma'am. Not til 7:30."

"Then whoever is on duty. Please, this is important." She turns again in a slow circle to look around her, but sees no one at all.

"This is Sergeant Dale. How can I help you?" The new voice is alert, and the caller instantly feels a connection.

"Sergeant, I'm in Romany Hill Park, on the south side near the ball field. I've found a stack of bags along the roadside that look to be full of money. I don't want to touch them, and I don't want to leave them."

"Yes, ma'am. I appreciate that. I've got a car on the way. Can you tell me how you happened to find them?"

"I was just finishing a run around the park like I do every morning about this time. I was walking to cool down when I saw these three bags."

"Three bags?"

"Yes. Neatly stacked near a trash can."

"And you stopped to investigate?"

"Yes."

"Why?"

"Well, I don't know. Just something about them made me look. I guess it was the way the sun hit the top one just right, and I could see it was money."

"And can I have your name, please?"

"King. Lissa King."

"Ms. King, there should be an officer there now."

Lissa looks around and sees the flashing blue lights of the white cruiser as it comes toward her. So much for keeping this quiet, she thinks.

"THIS MEAN ANYTHING TO YOU?" Captain Hutcheson handed a folded newspaper across the desk. Taking it, the other man read a brief account of the discovery of a large sum of money in garbage bags in a public park. Just 24 hours had passed since Lissa's discovery. The story, written in a slightly lighthearted vein, disclosed the facts more or less accurately. The reader's eyes stopped just for a second, at the name of the finder, before moving on. When he finished he handed the paper back to his superior.

"Nothing yet. I saw a reference to it in the daily report last week."

"Is that the same Lissa King, do you think?"

"No idea." Lieutenant Morris turned away and walked back to his own office. At least a week would go by before he could answer Hutcheson's question.

THE LOBBY OF MAIL & MORE WAS EMPTY, when Lissa walked in. From the counter area behind the boxes, David Horesh had looked around the corner at his customer. The tall, slender blonde looked familiar, but he couldn't quite place her.

"Hello," he said tentatively. "Can I help you?" His dark eyes, curly white hair and dark skin fit the slight accent that still held a suggestion of the Middle East.

"Mr. Horesh? Do you remember me? I'm Lissa King. I worked for you about a dozen years ago."

"Lissa! Of course!" The man came around the corner of the counter to take the young woman's hands in his. "How are you? Where have you been? What are you doing back in this small town? Back for a reunion?"

Lissa, as tall as the man, smiled, returned the warm hand clasp, and laughed. "Only a reunion here, Mr. Horesh. I've been out of the country for a while, and decided I missed this town. I'm here to stay, at least for now."

Horesh looked at her eyes, studied her for a moment. "Everything okay?" His voice was quieter, less emphatic. "You need a job?" He smiled at what he considered a joke.

"Actually, I could use something to do for now. I'm not destitute, but I could use something to do while I . . . while I find myself, I guess."

"Then you can start tomorrow! I have such a time getting people to work who are dependable, and care about the shop. I remember you were always the one I could count on. So start tomorrow, okay? Ah, I can't wait to tell Rachel!"

"Is she well? I often thought you two were so overworked."

"We are both fine. Getting older, trying to make a living, you know. But healthy, yes."

"It will be great to be back with you."

BY NINE O'CLOCK the next morning, Lissa was already sorting the day's mail, putting it in the boxes, when Rachel Horesh came in.

"Lissa," she said, with a laugh and a smile. "When David told me you were back, I couldn't believe it." Even more than 40 years in America had not taken the musical quality from the older woman's voice. She had changed, Lissa could see: no longer the dark and mysterious young woman from Iraq, but now matronly, well-fed, gray hair in a tight bun. Her voice was still warm and welcoming. The two women put their arms around each other and exchanged kisses on both cheeks. Standing back, Rachel held Lissa at arm's length and looked up at her. "A woman now, and so pretty! You have a husband and children, yes?"

"No. No, I'm still single, still alone. And no prospects," she offered, ahead of the question.

"When you graduated you were going to Washington, I remember. For graduate school, wasn't it?"

"It was, and I did and then stayed there for several more years. About a year ago I decided I needed a change. I've been out of the country, but I'm back now, and I just wanted to come to a place where I felt at home." As she listened to herself, she was pleased that her words sounded spontaneous and true.

"Oh, it's good to have you back. And David is so happy to have you in the shop again."

"At least for now," the younger woman offered. With no more questions, Rachel let her get back to her task, putting the incoming mail into the right private boxes, preparing outgoing mail for the postal service pick-up later in the morning, and through the day, dealing with customers coming in to leave packages for commercial pick-up, or to buy packing and shipping materials. The little shop stocked printer paper, provided copier services, and offered a small inventory of office supplies. Business, while steady, wasn't overwhelming.

A FEW DAYS AFTER SHE BEGAN WORKING, a man entered the store and went to the mailbox wall. A one-way glass separated that area from the rest of the store. He was swarthy, black curly hair, dressed in khaki trousers, a colorful sweater and a plaid shirt. She watched him open one of the boxes, then bend to look in, as if there might be something stuck in it, then snap the door closed. Turning to the one-way glass, he let his frown turn into a pleasant smile. He then walked to the doorway leading into the rest of the shop.

"Good morning. Can I help you?" Lissa came to the counter with what she hoped was a welcoming smile.

"Ah, yes. Hello. You are new here?" His voice, though not deep, was rich in tone and pleasant. "I've not seen you yet before." The voice had an accent that seemed to fit the odd sentence.

"I only started last week. But I used to work here a few years ago."

"al-Hasan. That's me. You are who?"

"Lissa, Mr. Hasan. Nice to meet you."

"al-Hasan. My last name. First name is Rizwan. Friends call me Zwani." He reached across the counter to shake hands. His palm was soft, damp, Lissa noted, the touch light and quick. "Then how my I help you Mr. al-Hasan?"

"The mail. Is it all in yet for today?"

"Yes, at least for the morning. If there is more we will get it in the afternoon, around two o'clock."

"I will come back." He smiled his open smile, turned and headed for the door. Turning before he opened it, he smiled again. "You take lunch with me perhaps?"

"Thanks, but I would have to close the store for that, and Mr. Horesh doesn't like to do that."

"Another time then?" He turned and left the shop.

"Are you charming, or what?" Lissa had said aloud. It was that encounter that prompted her to call Stan, and led to their first meeting since her return

STANLEY MORRIS REACHED ABSENT MINDEDLY for the cell phone buzzing in circles on his desk. He was intent on the final report he was writing, concluding a rather uninteresting investigation into fiscal malfeasance. Had the perp been a majority party member of the legislature, Stan thought, it would have been a quick and clean investigation. A plain John Doe citizen would have been slapped on the wrist, maybe spent an uncomfortable night in jail, and left to pick up his life. This legislator was not from the party currently in power, and that, of course meant a public and very noisy investigation, a trial and conviction . . . and then a slap on the wrist.

Catching the cell phone in mid-spin, he pressed the talk button without looking at the caller-ID information.

"Hello, Stan," said Lissa King.

Stan held the phone away from his ear, holding it and looking at it as if it were something that might spray water against his ear drum. He shook his head much as a swimmer might, coming up after a slow crawl across a pool.

"Lissa." It wasn't a question, it wasn't a response. If anything, it was an accusation. Of what? Suddenly all the parts began to reassemble. Lissa King who, for a few days a year and two months and three days and not many hours ago, had been a colleague, a lover, a killer, a . . . a great sadness in his life.

"Stan?" again.

"I'm here."

"Are you trying to tell me I shouldn't have called?"

A long pause, then: "No, no Lissa. Just taking me a moment to come back to today."

"From?"

A laugh. "From a year and two months and three days and," he paused, "and about six hours ago. Welcome home." *That's what you say to a returning warrior*, Stan thought.

"Thanks. I was hoping to hear that."

But was I? Hoping to hear that voice? Know she was okay, home again, near me? Stan's thoughts flashed back to the day they had parted at Dulles. She had stepped quickly away from the car, headed for he knew not where (did she?), leaving behind a dead Cold Warrior who had betrayed Lissa's agency and the country, escaping with only a denial by her chief that she even existed. Stan tried alternately to forget her and what he felt was love, and to remember this young woman who had invaded his professional and his personal life. In a way he resented the intrusion into both. As a former FBI agent, and now a State Police investigator, he had allowed this young woman to take his love, and to almost ruin his career. He knew she could provide a full measure of passion, and that she could also kill. She had killed Don Jackson, and she had wrapped her arms around Stan just as tightly as he had put his around her. To protect her if he could, to love her regardless. And now she had reappeared.

"Where are you? Alexandria?" He had a fleeting image of the sun-filled bedroom of her townhouse near the river. "Back in your house?"

"Not yet. For now I'm living in Beverley. I went to college here, and I guess I think of it as home." No response. "Can we meet?" She heard a long sigh. Maybe this wasn't such a good idea after all.

"I can be there in an hour."

THE DRIVE FROM SALEM took about half-an-hour longer than Stan had anticipated. As usual a tractor-trailer accident had closed I-81 near his exit, and the work-around on US 11 accounted for the delay. As he neared the town limits he used his hands–free to call the number Lissa's phone had left on his.

"There's a restaurant near where I'm living," she suggested. A neutral ground where they could meet. "It's in the old railroad station. Do you know where that is?"

Following her directions, he parked in front of the broad stairs leading to the Pullman Café. She was standing at the top of the wide, worn stone stairway. Stan sat for a moment, readying himself perhaps for what was to come. Then their eyes met, they smiled, he was out of the car taking the steps two at a time, as she came down to meet him half-way. Her lips, Stan thought, were just as he remembered them.

"Does Grady know you're back in the country?" They were sitting in a booth in the far corner of the still un-crowded dining room. The two dark beers they had ordered stood untasted. The empty platform beyond the big window was just beginning to fade into the shadow of evening. Lissa smiled at the question.

"I haven't seen him since I got back." Grady, head of internal security for the agency Don Jackson had betrayed, had told Stan to bury the story about Lissa's involvement in Jackson's death, that he would deny that she had ever been part of the agency. In the end the state's investigation concluded that the death had been "accidental, resulting from a self-inflicted wound." It was a large part of the dissatisfaction that shaped part of his relationship with this woman who had suddenly come back into his life.

The evening southbound Amtrak rumbled down the rails just outside the restaurant window. They both seemed relieved by the forced interruption. They watched silently as the conductor assisted an elderly couple up the steps, and the train prepared to continue its journey. Neither could think of anything to say. Finally the train started and slowly left the station taking its noise with it. The waiter hovered, waiting until Stan, with a nod of his head, said: "We're not ready to order yet. Give us a few minutes." He didn't look at the young man, but kept his eyes on Lissa.

After a rather vague description of where she had traveled during her year abroad, Lissa reached across the table and put one hand on Stan's. Before he could ask any more questions she began to speak, but not about travel.

"Stan, I'm sorry things happened the way they did. Sorry that you and I . . . that we weren't able . . . that we-weren't-able-to-work-things-out," she finished in a rush of words.

"Me too. Sorry that you couldn't tell me what was really going on."

"But I did, Stan. At the end."

"Yes. At the end. I just wish you could have confided in me sooner."

"Would you have helped me then?"

He didn't answer. He looked at her hand on his, looked into her eyes, looked out the window, then finally back to her face. "No. Maybe. I don't know. Lissa, I'm still a cop, and I can't . . . couldn't stop being one."

"I know. And that's part of why I called."

The waiter reappeared at Stan's elbow. His voice interrupted a silence. Both Lissa and Stan welcomed the distraction.

"I'll have the prime rib, very, very rare, the house salad and another draft," Lissa said, holding up her empty mug.

"The sirloin, very rare, house salad and another beer for me, too." Stan handed his menu to the waiter.

While they waited for their food, their conversation traveled other avenues.

Then: "Stan, I think I've stumbled into something."

"The money bags?"

"You know about that?"

"We read the papers, and the reports from around the state. Money interests us."

"The local people don't seem to be doing anything."

"What would you have them do?"

"Treasury? FBI? I don't know, but it seems too strange for three bags of new bills to be thrown away, and nobody wants them."

"Somebody wants them, Lissa, you can be sure of that. And somebody is looking at it. They are, we are, and the feds. So what did you have to tell me?"

"I think I may have a connection."

Stan looked around, aware of the waiter and the other people at tables near them.

"For now let's talk about something else, like why are you're really here, and how long you're going to stay?"

"I'm here, I guess, because I need to be somewhere, and because travel, while it makes you forget, doesn't make things go away."

"Things?"

"People. You." Her eyes held his. "I wanted to be with you again, Stan. I think," she added with a laugh, "I needed you."

"So why here? You know where my house is in Salem, and you knew where to find me. Why this town?"

"I went to college here, I remembered it as a friendly and interesting place, and if you didn't want me, I wouldn't be left on the sidewalk with my suitcase."

"I didn't leave you on the sidewalk, Lissa. I let you go at the airport. And it was your decision to leave, not mine."

"Would you have taken me in?"

Stan didn't answer. Instead he just let the silence push the conversation onto the next track.

"Anyway, I felt I needed to come back to someplace and that it should be a place I could feel at home. Beverley is it, for a lot of reasons. I have a nice place to live, right in the middle of downtown, near the college, and I even have a job."

"Let me guess: you've gone into business as a private eye."

"Almost as good: I'm managing a store that rents mailboxes and sells office supplies."

"Just what you were trained for, right?"

"I had worked there when I was in college."

"And the whole time you were away, you thought, 'Oh, I really need to go back to being a store manager in Beverley.'"

"Oh, Stan! Be serious."

"No, you be serious. Why are you here and why are you working in a store that provides blind mailboxes? Just a coincidence?"

"In a way it is. I came here because I know this town, I love its sense of place and history. The job isn't something I need, but after a few days, walking around, remembering the places I knew in college, I had used up my ability to do nothing. And I found myself in front of the store. I was surprised to find it still in business. I went in, just to see who owned it now.

AS THE MORNING SUN ILLUMINATED the brick sidewalks and intricately figured facades, Stan stood with a cup of coffee, watching the town come to life. Lissa, wrapped in a soft blanket, stood beside him, her head on his shoulder, relaxed she realized, for the first time since that winter day they had parted at the airport.

"Do you want to come by the shop before you leave? Maybe meet my boss?"

"I think I'll stay away from there for now."

"Do you think I'm wrong about this?"

"No. But if there is something, and my people want to get involved, I might not want to be connected yet. We don't do disguises, so showing my face too early might not be useful later.

"By the way, what about your boss, Horesch? His name's not on your list. He's from Iraq, isn't he?" Stan had been checking more than Lissa's list.

"He is, but not the right profile. He and his family, and all the other Jews in Iraq were thrown out by Saddam a long time ago."

Stepping away from the window, Stan finished dressing, caught Lissa up in his arms, let her know how much he wanted to stay, and left the apartment. She stood by the window, still in shadow, and watched him as he walked across the street to where he had parked the familiar black sedan. She couldn't tell if he looked up before driving away. She hoped he had.

JUST BEFORE NINE, LISSA UNLOCKED THE DOOR TO THE SHOP, stepped inside and began the day. First on her "to do" list was to open the access door to the back of the mailboxes, ready for the post office delivery. As she readied her cash register for the day, the first customer came in.

As he entered the combination to his box, Rizwan ibn al-Hasan seemed focused on what he was doing, but even to Lissa it was obvious that he was looking around, first at the door he had used to enter, then at the glass that obscured the woman watching him. When he had opened the door to his box he reached in, drew out the contents, quickly sorting them. He ran through the envelopes a second time. Shook his head, flipped the door closed, tossing the unopened mail into the waste basket next to the mailbox wall. Seeing no one, he looked toward the one-way glass, then walked to the part of the shop where Lissa stood.

"Hello, Lissa."

"Good morning Mr. al-Hasan."

"Please. Call me 'Zwani.' I see you every day now. We are friends." His smile was warm though his eyes weren't.

"I guess I try to maintain a business attitude, Mr. — Zwani."

He smiled. "That's more like it. So today we have lunch, yes?"

She smiled at his accent, and the way he put the words together. She had already arranged for Mr. Horesh to come in that morning, thinking it was time she accepted al-Hasan's invitation. "Well, as a matter of fact, I could do that," she smiled. "Come back at noon." The man's face lit up, even in his eyes.

"The mail. For today. It is in yet?"

"You're early, today." Lissa looked at the clock on the wall above the door. "It will be in at nine."

"Oh. I must come back, then, at noon." The man turned and walked out of the shop.

I wonder what you are expecting, Mr. al-Hasan, that after so many weeks of not checking your mail, you now come in every day. I don't really think it's my smile.

AT HIS OWN DESK, STAN WAS ON THE PHONE. The voice at the other end was barely audible to his chief who was standing beside him. As the conversation went on, Captain Hutcheson reached over and picked up a book lying on top of the desk.

"What can you tell me about him?" The voice at the other end rattled on. Stan made a note or two on a yellow pad, drawing arrows to another name already written there. "So he had been a pilot in your country? Why did he want to come here and take lessons?"

The other voice was less excited now, and still inaudible to the captain. Hutcheson flipped pages in the book he held, not really reading, but skimming quickly over the pages. The conversation didn't sound as if it were about to end, so he put the book down and walked slowly back to his own office across the hall.

Stan finished his conversation, snapped the phone closed. After he had made a few more notations on the pad he stared for a moment out the window behind him. Getting up, taking the pad with him, he crossed the hall to his superior's office.

Hutcheson, a man slightly older than Morris, was already showing the signs of too much desk time: jowls, a slight paunch, pale skin. His brown hair was thinning, the beginning of a widow's peak. He resembled a young Nixon, Stan thought, probably not as bright but just as tenacious. Tenacity was what had made him a good cop to begin with.

"What exactly are you working on, Morris? I couldn't help overhearing your conversation." He locked eyes with his lieutenant. "And what's that Koran book doing on your desk?"

"What I'm working on is a list of names I was given of people who might be from the Middle East, who might have something to do with 9-11.

As for the book, you know what it is, so why ask?"

"Well, I ask because I wonder what you're doing reading something like that, especially on company time. You want to read a bible, you don't need to spend time on that kind." Hutcheson's voice was sarcastic under the best of circumstances.

Stan said nothing, but returned his boss's stare. Then: "Called 'know your enemy,' Captain. We can't fight what we don't know."

"The New Testament's good enough for me, Morris. I don't want to see that trash in my space again. And if that girl's back in your life, I'll bet she's the one who got you onto this business."

"Why would you say that?"

"I know you went to see her last week, so I'm guessing she's got something to do with your sudden interest in religion."

"She wanted to know if we were doing anything about that money she found."

"So that was her. You didn't wait long to look her up."

"Actually, she called me."

"And you went running after her, is that it?"

"Just catching up, Hutch, that's all. I told her the feds were following the story."

"That's all?"

"She's also stumbled on a bunch of names of people who might be worth watching." Stan gave Hutcheson a brief description of where Lissa was working. The names were of renters who hadn't checked their boxes since just before 9-11. The names fit Middle Eastern patterns.

"Stan, if you want to go back to the FBI, fine. Just let me know. Otherwise, you keep focused on what happens in the state of Virginia that has to do with the state. Better let me have that list, and I'll pass it on to the right folks." He thrust his hand toward Morris. "And get that heathen book out of here." Obviously, Hutcheson's unhappiness with his subordinate's efforts had been working on his mind for some time. "If you don't have enough to do, I can reassign you to the road. Just tell me." Stan just looked at his chief, then went back to his office and retrieved the list he had been working from. He dropped it very carefully on the Captain's desk.

"From your 'mole'?"

She'll love that! A mole! Stan smiled. He crossed back to his own office. In his desk drawer lay the second copy of the list, and the notes he had already written about them. *I guess this will have to be my hobby. The advantage of being alone, I guess.* Stan didn't miss being married, no longer regretted that he and Theresa had parted years ago. Theresa, a forensic pathologist, had remarried, and now, when she was assigned to a case he was working, they were colleagues, not adversaries.

THE FARMLAND THAT SURROUNDS THE CITY of Beverley and its neighboring towns is wide and rich. Though turkeys and cattle predominate today, in the early years of settlement the upper Shenandoah Valley was recognized as the bread basket of America. Even today rich fields and remote farmsteads are a part of the Valley culture and experience. Outsiders can lose themselves here, relying on the respect for privacy to pursue lives as painters and writers and craftsmen of different art forms. And of course, like any truly rural part of the land, it is a place where people can hide in plain sight. Farmers in this area are aware of their neighbors, but seldom share that awareness with strangers.

It had taken Stan more than a few weeks to find the first link to a name on Lissa's list. It doesn't work if you simply go house to house asking if the person who answers the door knows someone named Abdul Hasib, or Tabassum or Dizhwar. Unless the one you are asking knows you, or has a complaint against the one you are looking for, you aren't likely to get more than a shake of the head, a drawling "no," or even a moment to consider the question. It didn't surprise him, but it was a little frustrating. About the third week of asking, he finally got a nod.

"Oh, yeah. Fellas that took the old Argenbrite place over by Stringtown. Don't see 'em often, but one was at the store couple days ago when the missus and I stopped for gas. We were on our way to town, going shopping." The man looked off to the north, vaguely in the direction of that city about 20 miles away. "Don't know his name, but that's who you're asking about, I betcha."

The farm was one of the larger ones in the valley. Large but generally out of production. From the highway, on a slight elevation, Stan could see the fence lines, the barns and other outbuildings, and a square, two-story house that sat near the road. With his binoculars he scanned the spread. Except for a long swath in a large pasture near one of the barns, the fields had been allowed to grow up, fallow but still productive, though wild. But that long well-mowed and clear looking flat strip, maybe a couple of thousand feet long, leading from one of the barns: that was interesting. As he swept the area again he noticed, on the ridge of the barn roof, an orange flag flapping in the light breeze. A gust and he saw that it was a windsock. That would explain the well-groomed field. He put the car in gear, and headed back to Beverley, and to Lissa.

STAN WAS SITTING AT THE ROUND TABLE near the window, watching Lissa as she moved between stove and counter and refrigerator. Her body silhouetted by the morning sun, he admired the economy of motion, the sureness with which her hands worked over the omelet she was preparing.

Eggs, blended with a few strokes of a whisk, onions and tomatoes and peppers cut, chopped fine, seasoned and stirred into the eggs. The mix slid into the pan, a low flame releasing the wonderful scent. Now a quick motion of her fingers to crumble the rich goat cheese and fold it into the eggs. Another quick motion, the omelet flipped up and dropped neatly back into the pan, and it was done.

"Where are we going with this, Lissa? Do you have any idea about it?"

"No, not really. I mean, I see that something is happening, that there are some bad people out there doing what might be bad things, but I can't see what it is. Are they planning another raid, like in September, or are they just holding themselves ready for orders from somewhere else? Stan, I don't have any idea." She walked over to the table with the plates. "But you were out driving around yesterday you said, and you haven't told me what you found."

"Only some curiosities."

"Tell me."

Stan thought for a minute about what he had seen the day before. "A farm, mostly abandoned looking, rented to people who could be on your list. A barn, a windsock, a well-mowed piece of pasture, long and narrow like a landing field. Maybe an airplane in the barn. Comments from neighbors who have only seen the occupants, but never met them. That's all I've got so far."

"Are you going to set up a watch?"

"Lissa, I'm already in trouble with my chief over the list of names you gave me. What I did yesterday was just something I can do on my day off. When I go back to Salem, I leave all this behind. You understand?"

"I do. And Stan," she moved to his side, knelt and put her arms around him, "I really appreciate your taking this on for me. It means a lot that you would do it."

Before returning to Salem, Stan agreed to drive Lissa out into the county to show her the farm. From the highway, using Stan's powerful binoculars, she studied the front of the house. She was rewarded with the image of al-Hasan as he opened the door.

FOUR DAYS LATER, ZWANI AND LISSA SAT IN A BOOTH along the wall of the pizzeria. As they ate the vegetarian pizza he talked of growing up as the son of a wealthy and respected clan leader. He spoke little of politics and wars, focusing on how his world had expanded by coming to America for school, and the contrasts he saw when he did visit his family. In spite of her misgivings, Lissa enjoyed her conversations with this reserved, obviously intelligent man. But there was an anger she could sense, often just below the surface.

"The world is an evil place," he would often say. "People must learn to live according to God's law."

"Do you think there is only one way, one god?"

"Of course, Lissa: My god." Then he would smile, and change the subject. Lissa didn't pursue it. She wasn't afraid of him. She simply wasn't ready to confront him, so she focused on other things. Though she tried to lead him in conversations about what he was doing in Beverley, in America for that matter, she didn't push, hoping he would open to her over time. But did she have time?

THEY MET FOR LUNCH several times over the next few weeks, but they saw each other every day when he came in to check his mail. It was still mostly circulars, "Flying" magazine, and an occasional letter from an al-Hasan in

Beirut. "Letter from home," he would say, smiling, waving the letter toward the window where he knew Lissa would be watching. Those he would open immediately, and sometimes come around the partition and share excerpts from his letters: a sister having a baby, his mother's health, his brother's efforts to expand the family business. Often his openness was disarming, but the anger was still there.

"When are you going back?"

"When? I don't know. It depends on how things go at home. I'm not sure."

"Don't you want to go back? Or," she added with a laugh, "did you do something so terrible they don't want you back?"

"What do you mean?" His face showed the anger more than his voice. "I'm here because I want to be here!" He sat back in the booth, the anger that had flared in his eyes now cooled. "You wouldn't understand, Lissa. Your country and mine, we are so different, want different things."

"What kind of things?" Lissa didn't want a debate. She posed questions that she hoped would let Zwani open his thinking to her.

"There is too much license here, too much what you call 'personal freedom.' In my country we would never be allowed to meet like this, without relatives around."

"A sort of chador curtain?"

"You think that is funny, yes? But it is necessary. Too many girls have been ruined when they drop the veil."

"But you seem to approve of that just by sitting here with me, Zwani."

"Yes, but you have too much freedom, I think." Sliding out of the booth, he stood over her. "It is time I took you back to your work," he said, less angry now, but still not completely cooled down. "Must not keep the old Je - - man in his store too long."

Almost called him the "old Jew," didn't you? How sad to have such confusion in your life. Doing business, even through me, with a people you hate so much.

Lissa and al-Hasan walked silently back to the store. *And what do you want from me?*

IN THE LATE AFTERNOON LIGHT, the old brick and stone facade of the building glowed warmly. Inset in the wall near the corner of the building was a full-pane door, and behind that, the stairway to the second floor and Lissa's loft. As she approached the door she saw a flicker of movement in the darkened hallway. Immediately on guard, she swung her shoulder bag so that it was behind her, freeing her hands and at the same time making it easy to drop the bag if it got in her way. Pushing against the old door, she opened it, then took a step back. A hand thrust out from the darkness, but her movement avoided the grasp that was obviously intended to drag her inside. The door was yanked open, and a man she didn't know came through the door in a rush. He was not quite as tall as al-Hasan, but like him: swarthy, hair and beard curly and black. The man's momentum sent him past Lissa and as she put a foot out to trip him, he fell to the sidewalk. Just as quickly, Lissa stepped through the door, slammed it behind her, and turned the deadbolt lock. Through the glass she could see the man rising painfully from the sidewalk, and at least two people stopping to help him. As she retreated up the stairs she saw him shake off the helping hands, turn glaringly to the door and then walk stiffly and quickly away.

"Stan, I think I was almost grabbed a minute ago." Coldly, Lissa assessed the interrupted attack even as Stan Morris was hearing her first

189

words.

"You okay?"

"Yes. Fine. He was an amateur."

"Recognize him? Did you get a look at him?" Stan's voice was calm but not cold. Being lover and policeman was a difficult balance at the best of times, but he managed it. Hutcheson, who lately seemed to hover near Stan's door, stopped what he was doing to listen.

Lissa related the details of the near-miss and described the would-be attacker. "About 5 feet six or seven, dark skin, dark eyes, thick curly black hair, muscular but slow on his feet." She ended with a laugh. In anyone else, Stan would have said a "nervous" laugh, but not from this woman. She was very much in control, and any breathlessness would have been from running up the stairs to her steel-doored loft.

"I've got pictures now, to go with the names. I'll forward them. See if you can pick out your man."

After agreeing to meet for dinner, Morris broke off the conversation. Turning to his captain, as he put the phone down on the desk, he just looked at him, saying nothing. Hutcheson, standing in the doorway, shook his head and walked away. Resigned to his subordinate's independence, accepting his sometimes unorthodox way of solving cases, he had given up trying to push his man too far. After all, his department's success rate determined his own. He trusted his man, and that was that. Besides, his department's success affected his wallet.

THEY WERE SITTING IN WHAT HAD BECOME "their" booth. Alex, the waiter who always served them, knew enough to interrupt them only when the conversation had ceased. As they sipped their beers they looked at the pictures Stan had brought with him; duplicates of the ones Lissa had seen on her computer earlier.

"So you are certain this is the one?" Stan put his finger on the picture that topped the pile. "Another 'student,' I see. Wonder what these boys are studying that takes so long?"

"The college may have records of them," Lissa offered. "I don't have a license to ask, but you do. Could you try? There aren't too many schools around here for people of his age or background." The men had all been here for three or more years, on student visas, and in the case of at least two of them, their visas had run out. Her attacker was one of those.

"I'll look at that. Draw a 30-mile circle and you have three universities and several community colleges, as well as vocational schools. Their visa applications should give me a starting point. The question to ask is 'are they still students?'"

"And just what are they studying? Zwani . . . al-Hasan . . . seems to have a lot of time on his hands."

"Suwannee? Like the river?"

"Zwani, with a 'z.' It's what his friends call him."

"You're his friend?" Stan's tone was speculative and immediately distant.

"We've had lunch a few times. I'm hoping he will confide in me at least a little. He's already told me that he's been taking flying lessons at the airport."

Stan sat back against the cushion of the booth. He studied Lissa for a moment. Then: "I think you know more about these men than you're telling me, Lissa."

"More? What kind of more is there?"

"Well, there's all kinds of 'more,' I guess, but my thoughts run to more as in 'more than superficial interest.' Lissa," he paused, "why don't you tell me exactly what you are doing in all of this?"

Glancing up, Lissa saw Alex, menus in hand, approaching the table. "Not now, not here, Stan." Smiling up at the waiter, she said, "I know what I want, Alex."

The conversation continued, but Lissa deftly steered it away from Stan's question. Using her knife and fork, she surgically parted the meat from the sparerib bones. As she lifted the last bite, she looked up from her plate to Stan and then, almost suddenly, to a place behind him. Stan turned to follow her gaze as she slid further into the booth to make room for the man who turned and slid in beside her. "I know you remember Mr. Grady, Stan."

BY THE TIME STAN LEFT to return to Salem, it was nearly mid-night. Grady had already taken himself off to the guest room in the loft. Lissa, hoping to find peace in sleep was still upset by the abrupt and angry but ultimately accepting response Stan had to Grady's appearance. Her own sleep was fitful and disturbed, mostly by a dream that included snatches of forgotten conversations with Stan that seemed to be about the first time they worked together.

"It's a good thing I don't have nosey neighbors," Lissa said as she prepared breakfast for herself and her guest in the morning. "All these men coming and going at all hours! What must they think?"

Grady grumbled a laugh before adding, "Just tell 'em I'm your uncle."

"Uh huh. And Stan is my brother and the guy in the doorway was just passing through. Or maybe I'm operating a B&B without a license."

"Good cover." Grady wasn't a talkative man in the best of times, and especially not at breakfast.

"Funny."

"My wife thinks I am."

"You've got a wife?" Lissa said in mock surprise. "Why Mr. Grady, you never stop surprising me. Like last night, showing up in our hideaway without warning."

"Lissa, I told you when you started on this assignment that I'd let you do it your way until I thought it was time to step in. That attack yesterday was time. I think your friend, Mr. al-Hasan, may know more about you than you are willing to admit to yourself. And I don't want to have to explain to your Lieutenant Morris why I didn't protect you better."

"Mr. Grady, we're so close now. To the end, I mean. I have thought for the last week or so that al-Hasan was about to confide in me. I don't want to interrupt that trust now. We're almost there."

"Like Morris, I want to know where 'there' is, Lissa. Do you know?"

"I don't know. My guess is that Zwani – al-Hasan – thinks I will help him do what he wants."

"So what was that guy doing in your doorway?"

"Maybe he was trying to scare me so that al-Hasan can push me to help him."

Grady, Morris and King had talked the night before about the barn with a windsock. And the fact that the time limit for someone to claim the bags of money was almost up.

"I think Zwani is expecting me to be awarded the money. I think he wants to pull me in so that I will give it to him. I think the men are planning to buy a small plane, bring it to the farm they rent, load it with something terrible, and make another attempt at the White House or the Capitol. That's what I think."

Grady looked at his young assistant. He saw, beyond the innocent face, an eager operative. He saw a fire in her eyes, ignited by a sense of mission, of the need to protect. He had seen it in her when he hired her, before she took on the assignment of identifying and neutralizing a turncoat in their own organization: the man who had caused the death of her own father. Now she was taking on a much wider, deeper threat. And she was ready to give everything she had.

"What about Morris?" the question was simple.

"He's in."

"Not what I meant, King. What about him?"

"I'm yours first, Mr. Grady. Yours and the agency. Anything, anyone else, is not really a factor beyond that."

"I don't think I really believe that."

"You'll just have to, I guess."

It was just after sunrise when Grady left the apartment. An hour later Lissa was on her way to the Horesh's store.

STAN WAS IN FRONT of Hutcheson's desk. "I think you ought to know what happened yesterday – what's been going on." Generally considered a loaner, Morris was not at all easy about explaining his relationship with Lissa and her work. "There seem to be some people operating out of Beverley who might have a possible link to either 9/11, or the people who sponsored it. That's what we've been talking about – King and I. And then there's this man Grady. Seems that what we thought happened last time, about her leaving the country, well . . . it wasn't true. Or if it was, it was part of a plan." Stan ran his finger around the collar of his shirt. The chill in the office didn't reach him at all. "So . . . so I need to keep going with this now." He stopped. He looked at Hutcheson.

"Yeah. Grady called me a week ago. Read me in. Said it was national security and all that. Still don't know as I believe him or trust him. These Feds can do some pretty foolish stuff now and then."

SOON AFTER SHE OPENED that morning, Zwani came in, coming directly to the counter instead of first checking his mailbox.

"You are okay this morning?" His face seemed darker than usual, Lissa thought.

"Just fine, Zwani. And you?"

"Okay. I'm okay too."

"Good." Lissa smiled, hoping her increased awareness didn't show.

"I wonder if we could have dinner together tonight, Lissa. There are some things I would like to talk about."

LISSA WAS DOWNSTAIRS in the small vestibule between the street door and the stairway when Zwani pulled up at the curb. The car was an unremarkable sedan with New Jersey plates, clean but not very new. Its silver color would be hard to distinguish from the hundreds of similarly colored cars so popular at the time. Before he could get out of the car Lissa was at the door, and quickly got in.

"Can't park on this side," she said. "Wouldn't want you to get a ticket."

Zwani reached over, opened the glove box and pointed to a thick pile of paper. "I just stick them in there," he laughed. "Someday I must pay them, I guess."

"I guess so."

The car pulled smoothly back into the leisurely flow of traffic and in a few minutes they were headed out of town.

"Where are we going?" Lissa put what she hoped was anticipation into her question.

"I am cooking you at my house dinner," he said, "because I want us to be alone. You don't mind?"

"Of course not, Zwani. I'm intrigued. I didn't know you were a chef."

"Not me. I have good friend staying for a while. Very excellent at making food from our country. I think you will be surprised."

"Depends on what's cooking." Lissa wondered if al-Hasan understood the full meaning of that American slang.

"Well, I let you be surprised."

Maybe he does understand it. She moved her purse, comforted by the extra weight it carried.

When the car came to a stop at the front door of the farmhouse, Lissa waited for Zwani to come around and open the door for her.

In the front hall al-Hasan helped her with her coat, then picked up her purse and started to open a closet door.

"I'll keep my purse, Zwani. A girl never likes to be too far from her lipstick."

"But you don't wear lipstick, Lissa. That's one of your charms." He hung the coat on a hanger and started to put her purse on a shelf.

"Shows how observant you are, my friend. You can't tell if I do it right." She stepped forward and took the purse from him.

"It seems heavy for lipstick."

"I guess it must, to a man."

"Well, come into the livingroom. I will tell Dizhwar we are here. It will take only a little time to finish his preparations." He walked through a swinging door leading into the kitchen. Lissa caught just a glimpse of the man at the stove when he turned toward al-Hasan. He was short, solid, dark. He was the man in the doorway. Lissa pulled her purse closer.

Coming back to the livingroom, bringing two glasses of orange juice, Zwani offered one to his guest. Lissa took hers, and while they talked of meaningless things, like the age of the house and the comforts it offered, she sipped the sweet drink. It seemed a little less tart than the orange juice she was used to. Her lack of enthusiasm for it must have been obvious.

"You don't care for the juice? I can get you something else."

"The juice is fine, Zwani. I just want to be sure I have an appetite to match the wonderful smells coming from the kitchen." Her host nodded, accepting her words.

"Dizhwar is a wonderful chef. In our country he had his own restaurant." He laughed, patting his stomach. "Here I am almost his only customer, and it is beginning to show."

"Did Dizhwar come here to study cooking?" Lissa looked at her host over the rim of her glass which she still held close to her lips.

"He wanted to learn how to take care of large groups of people," was the enigmatic reply.

"Where is he studying?"

"Right now he is out of school. It is a question of money, you see."

"And that is what you are looking for in the mail?" Her host's eyes closed briefly, then opened again as he looked at her.

"Always letter from home. Telling where money is being sent is always good to know."

As he finished speaking the door to the kitchen swung open. "Ready," said Dizhwar, and turned back to the kitchen. Al-Hasan stood and offered his hand to Lissa. Still holding the glass, she stood and accompanied her host to the dining room. He seated her with her back to the kitchen and seated himself across from her. A third place was set for Zwani's house mate. Settled in their chairs, the door to the kitchen opened and Dizhwar brought in a tray with three bowls of tomato and chickpea soup. He put them down and took his seat between Lissa and al-Hasan. Zwani introduced him to Lissa. Smiling as she acknowledged the introduction, she looked at the chef and said, "I think we have met before. You must have come into the shop at some time." She smiled and turned her attention to the soup. Maybe it wasn't so smart to let him know that, Lissa thought. On the other hand, it might make my being here less awkward for us both.

Dizhwar, still hurting from his fall, concentrated on the soup. As soon as the bowls were empty he returned to the kitchen and brought out two platters of kebabs. Finely cut pieces of lamb, prepared in a spicy marinade, and on a separate platter, vegetable kebabs of tomatoes, onions, red and green bell peppers. To Lissa the food was exotic, appetizing and, when she tasted it, met every expectation the aroma promised.

As they ate, Zwani and Lissa commented on the food. Dizhwar said nothing. He ate quickly, in the traditional manner using the fingers of his right hand. Her host, Lissa saw, perhaps in deference to his guest, used a fork as she did. She talked little, concentrating on the food until she felt she could eat nothing more. When all had finished, Dizhwar rose from the table and began collecting the empty platters and plates.

"Can I help?" Lissa began to feel an empathy with the man who had prepared such a feast, even to the point of wondering if perhaps she had misjudged his intent when she saw him behind the door to her building. Was he just waiting with a message from Zwani, she wondered?

"No, no. Thank you." He nodded his head, turned and left the room. She heard the door swing open and closed.

"I can understand why you like having your friend here. Do you eat like this every night?"

"Yes, I'm afraid we do." Zwani smiled, patted his generous stomach, and added: "I eat far too well with him here."

Dizhwar returned now with a platter of sweet smelling baklava and a coffee pot. The liquid he poured was strong, very black and aromatic. Eyeing the dessert, Lissa mentally counted the calories and politely refused. Coffee, on the other hand, was just what she needed. The food had sated her, and she felt in need of the jolt caffeine would give her. Surprisingly, as the conversation with Zwani ranged over a wide but noncontroversial spectrum, she felt herself growing more relaxed, even sleepy. When Dizhwar left the table again, she wondered vaguely what he might be bringing to the table next.

The door swung in, and she sensed the man from the kitchen coming in, but was unable to respond when what she thought was a thick loop of rope came over her and down, pulling tight to bind her to the chair.

WHEN LISSA AWOKE she realized she was in a small room. Her head was remarkably clear but her arms and legs felt stiff and immobilized. Her clothes, though still on, were in some disarray. Obviously she had been searched, and just as surely, they had found the wire she had been wearing. She lay back, wondering what the time was, and what options she had. Depending on what her captors wanted, she might have no time at all, or perhaps all the time in the world.

The door opened slowly. In the light from the hallway she knew that Zwani was there. He entered the room, followed by Dizhwar. The other man carried a tray and as he came closer she could see that it held a coffee pot and a cup.

Zwani smiled down at her. "You must have been very tired after that fine meal. You suddenly fell asleep, right at the table. I expect you have been working too hard. I hope you don't mind that we brought you here to our guest room? You nearly fell from your chair." His voice was solicitous and the tone tried to say he really cared, but Lissa knew better.

"I apologize, Zwani. I don't usually respond to my host like that." She raised her head, and tried to sit up. He slipped an arm behind her and helped her to sit.

"Try this coffee. It should help. Dizhwar makes it very strong." He let her take the cup, and she drank it slowly.

"Oh, that's so much better. I was so dry. I really can't imagine what happened to me. You must think I'm a terrible guest." Lissa sat up now, looked around her. "I must look a mess. Did you think to bring my purse too?" She smiled what she hoped was a winning smile.

Her host reached down beside the bed and lifted her shoulder bag from the floor beside the bed. "I know you don't like to be separated from this," he said with a smile. He handed it to her. Immediately she realized it was lighter than it should be. Zwani reached behind him and brought her Smith and Wesson .38 Special from his back pocket. "I took the liberty of removing this. It is what made your bag so heavy." He smiled. "Do you always take this when you go out to dinner with a man?"

"Of course." Lissa smiled.

"But it seems so unladylike, such a weapon. Can you use it?" He handed it to her. "I removed the bullets so you wouldn't hurt yourself."

"You know how Americans are about guns. We learn to use them very early."

Fully awake now, Lissa turned and put her feet on the floor. Without difficulty she stood and picked up her bag. "I think I'd better be going, now. You've taken more than enough trouble, and I'm deeply embarrassed to have had this little episode."

"Sit down, Lissa." The voice was no longer sugary and nice, but peremptory. "We have things to discuss."

AGAINST THE NIGHT SKY the black Crown Victoria was nearly invisible. Originally a silver and blue state police cruiser, the car was still equipped with switches that prevented the interior lights from coming on when the doors opened, with a spot light, and even a built-in rack for two-way radios and a laptop. A mount for a shotgun also took up part of the front seat space. Seated behind the wheel, Stan Morris made a minor adjustment to the radio receiver beside him, rotating a roof-top antenna slightly to improve reception. The ear bud he wore relayed the conversation at the dinner table. The microphone, cunningly secreted in an ordinary ballpoint pen clipped to the outside pocket of Lissa's shoulder bag, let Stan know that she was not only okay, but that she was being very well fed. Holding a not very warm cheeseburger in his hand, he endured the glowing food review being provided by the three at the table in the house just down hill from Stan's car, hidden by the overgrown weeds along the roadside. He folded up the paper and thrust the half-eaten burger back into its paper bag. At least the coffee in his cup was still hot.

"This better pay off, Lissa, or I'm going to let you buy me the best dinner in town when we get back!" She couldn't hear him, of course, and Stan knew that, but he felt better having said it. Lissa's voice in his ear recalled him to the present.

"Uhhh," in fact was Lissa's voice, trailing off suddenly. Stan was instantly alert. That wasn't a conversational gambit, he could tell. The next words he heard were in a language he didn't speak or understand. The voices were al-Hasan and his partner. Lissa was silent. The sounds faded. After a brief silence he heard the two again, approaching the microphone. He heard footsteps and a door open and close.

Had it been anyone else, Stan probably would have been on his way to the door of the house. Not hearing Lissa's voice, but only those of the two men speaking in what he identified as Arabic, he was torn between breaking into the house and letting her work it out on her own. He waited.

After an agonizing quarter of an hour, during which he heard only muffled conversation between the two men, there was finally a sound he recognized as coming from Lissa. Not words so much as the sound one makes when awakening from a very deep sleep. More breath sounds than words. Enough to let him know she was at least alive, but he had never doubted that for an instant. Even at this point in their investigation, both Stan and Lissa knew that whatever the men were planning, Lissa alive was something they were counting on. He heard a door open.

"You must have been very tired after that fine meal. You suddenly fell asleep, right at the table. I expect you have been working too hard. I hope you don't mind that we brought you here to our guest room? You nearly fell from your chair."

Hearing the conversation reassured Stan, and he returned to listening mode. Action would have to wait.

"Sit down, Lissa. We have things to discuss."

"I can't think of any," she countered. "I really need to go home." There was just a slight hint of emotion in her voice, but Stan knew her well enough to believe it was done for effect.

"There is this." al-Hasan reached into his shirt pocket and drew out the miniature recorder. "You will forgive me, but it was necessary to search you when we brought you here. In your under-garments we found this. I think it is called a 'wire,' isn't it?"

Her hand fluttered to her breast, acknowledging that the device had been hers.

"Only to search you, not to fondle," Dizhwar said in his guttural voice.

Thanks for that reassurance, she thought. Then: "Oh, you found that." She offered what she hoped was a weak but reassuring smile.

The man waited for further explanation but none came. "You are from the police."

"The police? Certainly not. No."

"Why you wear this then?"

"I don't think I should tell you." They were standing nearly face-to-face. The man put his hand on her shoulder and pushed her back until she sat again on the edge of the bed. *I know I can take you down when I'm ready, but let's just play this out some more.* She offered what she hoped was a surprised look.

"Talk to me about this, Lissa, or I will have to think the worst."

"And what would the worst be, Mr. al-Hasan?"

"That you are police, and that America doesn't trust me because I come from Middle East." He sat now on the chair beside the bed, his hands on his knees, leaning close to her. His companion stood to the side, his hands empty of the tray, open, ready.

"I found some money." Lissa sat forward in a defensive position, her balance toward her questioner. "It was quite a lot of money, and I turned it in to the police."

Zwani nodded his head. "Of course. We know that. It was in the papers."

"The police think whoever the money belongs to will try to contact me." She pointed to the recorder. "They asked me to wear that just in case."

"And you think it is me?"

"I have no idea, Zwani. I just wear it all the time, and once a day a policeman comes and we exchange them so they can listen to what I recorded. Everyday," she added for emphasis. "So I am just in the habit. Please don't take offense." Her eyes pleaded with both men. "Why would I think it is you?"

Al-Hasan sat back in his chair. *Good. So far he believes me.*

"I don't know. Why would you?"

204

"But I don't, Zwani, I really don't have any idea who owns that money. And in a week, if no one claims it, it will come to me."

"I don't believe you, Lissa. I think you know that is my money."

"Then why haven't you claimed it?"

"You not a stupid person, Lissa. You find a couple of bags with money. You don't pick up and run away, you call police. You look around to see anybody watching."

"You were there?" Her question was delivered as innocently as she could make it.

"Not ten meters away."

"Oh."

"Then you call and police come."

"And you read my name in the paper."

"And I find you. Now, you nice girl, Lissa. Smart, too I think. So I tell you what."

"What?"

"What you going to do. You are going to wait until police give you money, then you give to me. You say nothing to nobody. Just do as I say and we be okay."

"What's the money for, Zwani?"

"For me. For my friends. From my friends who help me."

"Why can't they just send you a check?"

"You ask too much questions."

You certainly do, my girl. Just say yes, and get up and get out of there. The sun is about to come up and I need to be out of sight, which means out of range, and that is beyond this microphone's range. Morris moved in the cramped seat, paying attention for the first time to his stiff and cramped muscles.

"If the money is yours, then I'll give it to you, of course, Zwani. I wouldn't want something that doesn't belong to me. But how can I know that you are telling the truth?"

"You must trust me." He leaned forward, trying to project sincerity. "I would not lie to you. That would be dishonorable."

"But you have lied to me, haven't you? You only sought me out because of the story in the paper."

"But I have come to like you, Lissa, and I don't want you to be hurt. Now say yes and I will take you home." He reached across and took the revolver she had put beside her on the bed. "I keep this now. It is too big for a girl."

Oh, if you only knew, Stan said aloud.

"Please. That belonged to my father. It is the only thing I have of his," she ended almost in a whisper.

"I keep for now. I give you back this." He handed her the recorder. "It has been off since we found it. You will not tell the police about our 'discussion,' I think?"

"No, I'll say nothing. But you must bring me some proof that the money is yours."

"When you give it to me, I will. Now it is time to go home."

I THINK WE'D BETTER FIND SOME OTHER PLACE to meet," Stan said. At this early hour he was alone in his office. "Your dinner companions are probably watching your building."

"Maybe we shouldn't meet at all until this is over."

"Then we need to close it out soon. I don't want too much time to go by without seeing you."

"That's the nicest compliment you've paid me, Stan." Lissa felt suddenly warmed by an emotional response to his words.

"I've worked out with the local cops how to deliver the money to you." Stan returned to business. Switching the phone to his left hand, he picked up a piece of paper from his desk. "One of the municipal court judges will sign the order tomorrow, awarding you the funds. There is a fee to cover costs of the court, but other than that, you will have nearly $200-thousand to give to Mr. al-Hasan."

"That should make him happy, Stan. But what then? I just hand it over and he runs off to Wal-Mart? I mean, what's he going to do with it? You can't put a wire in the bag!"

"Grady and I are taking care of that. The money is traceable, for one thing. The bills are large enough to be noticed"

"Suppose he ships it out of the country?"

"We're counting on that not happening. Grady says it came from outside the country in the first place."

"He hasn't told me that. How does he know?"

"Treasury knows where the bills went when they left the Mint."

"You and Grady seem to be getting on well." Lissa's voice let Stan know she felt left out.

"This is an operation, Lissa. It carries some risk. We need to manage that risk as much as we can." Silence followed. Then: "I want to minimize the risk, Lissa." His tone was soft, quiet.

"Should I call Zwani and tell him I will have the money tomorrow?"

"No. Let's get it in your hands first. Did he come into the shop today?"

"Yes. We were civil, but otherwise he said little and I said nothing."

"Okay. At this point, probably the less said and so on. Just keep him on the right side of the edge." The conversation ended with instructions to wait for the local police to deliver the money.

A WEEK LATER, A POLICE CAR PULLED UP IN FRONT OF THE STORE just after Lissa opened. The sergeant who came in was carrying a large cardboard box. The papers attached to it, and the seals and signatures on it, indicated that it had been held in custody by the Beverley police department, that it had been delivered to the court and retrieved.

"Well, Miss King, here's your Christmas present. A little early, maybe, but the judge says it's all yours. Less a bit for the state, you understand, and for the court and for us."

"For you, too? The department, I mean?"

"Rules of the house," he said, as Lissa signed a receipt. "Call it a storage fee, if you like. Still, it's a good piece of change: just under $200-thousand. Maybe you could buy Mr. Horesh out." He laughed, wished her good luck and turned to leave. "Oh," said, as he opened the door, "we didn't put a wire in the box, just in case you wondered." He closed the door behind

UNUSUAL SUSPECTS – Four Stories

him, and Lissa watched as he drove away.

"It is here, I see." Rizwan al-Hasan came through the door and closed it quietly behind him. "That was simple, I hope."

Lissa had picked up the box and was putting it in the big safe standing at the back of the room. Al-Hasan started toward her, but she closed the door and turned the wheel, locking it, before he could reach her. He was close behind her when she turned to put out a hand, palm out, chest high. "Not yours yet, Mr. al-Hasan."

"Lissa! Why so formal? We are partners, you and I, yes?" The smile was temporary. "Open the safe and give me the box."

"You said you would prove it was yours. Do it."

The man started to put a hand out, aimed at her breast. "Still wearing your special jewelry?" Lissa's raised arm nearly knocked Zwani off balance when it swept his hand away. "You are strong, hey?"

"I'm sorry, Zwani. I don't like to be touched, even in fun. And you said you would tell me. I'm waiting." The outer door opened, and Dizhwar came in. He closed the door behind him and locked it.

"Do you know what Dizhwar's name means? It translates as 'mean' or 'strong.' And, I'm sorry to say, it fits him very well."

"Are you trying to scare me, Zwani?"

"Now, now, Lissa. Don't get excited. I think you are strong for a girl, and you like to play, but you just a girl, you know? You let me take care of this, okay? You don't need worry about money, things like that."

"You don't understand, do you? It isn't the money, so much as your promise." Lissa seemed to back away, though there wasn't really anyplace for her to go. "I'm serious about knowing that it is yours. You could be anybody, just reading the paper and thinking you could get this money from me. Why shouldn't I keep it for myself?"

Al-Hasan stepped back from the girl, looked around, and seeing no one except Dizhwar, nodded his head. "Okay, little girl. This has gone on long enough. That money is for us, it comes from our family in Iraq, and it has a purpose. You can give me the money and go away, or you can join us and help do something very important for our country, and" in a deliberate afterthought, "for yours. Wouldn't you like to do that? To help your country?"

Of course I would, Zwani. If I know what it is, and how it will help.""

"No, no. Don't need worry yourself about that. I say it will, it will. You let Zwani look after you, okay?"

"I don't need you to look after me, really."

"You got no father, so who? You got a brother maybe? Where is he?"

In her heart she was furious with herself for allowing this man to think she needed anyone to "take care of her."

"In my country you would not be allowed to even have this little job, you know? We take care of our women."

"Yes, I've heard that." *I've heard how you take care of 'your women,' Mr. al-Hasan, and we've all seen how you value life, so let's get this over with.*

"Now, open the safe like a good girl, and we will finish our business here today."

"Oh, but I can't, Zwani. Only Mr. Horesh has the combination. I asked him to open if for me this morning, because I knew the money was coming in, and I wanted to be sure it was safe."

Al-Hasan's face went from bland to brutal in a second. "Don't lie to me, Lissa. Open the safe and get the money out, or I will ask Dizhwar to 'help' you. Do it now!"

"Zwani, you frighten me when you talk like that. I can't open the safe. Besides, you still haven't proven that the money is yours." At that moment the front door darkened, the light blocked by a tall man trying to open it. "Now I'm going to unlock the door and let the customer in." Lissa walked around the end of the counter and headed toward the door. "Otherwise he might think something is wrong and call the police. You don't want that, I think."

Lissa unlocked the door. "Sorry. The lock must have snapped when the last customer went out." Stan smiled and entered the store.

"I just need some copy paper. What kind do you have?" He walked to the counter, nodded to the two men looking at the mailboxes, and faced Lissa. Dizhwar and al-Hasan left the store and walked down the street.

"What are you looking for from them, Lissa?"

"Any correspondence or documents that will give us a name or address outside the country. Grady is ready to pick them up as soon as we have something."

"Better sell me some paper and I'll leave. Is the back door unlocked?"

"Yes. It leads to the office."

"Is the office unlocked? I'll come in and be there."

"Stan, if al-Hasan wants me to go with him, I will. If he can't show

211

me what he has here, he may say that I need to come with him and he will prove his ownership. I've got to go if that is what he wants." Stan looked at Lissa for a long moment, before agreeing.

"If you do, you won't be alone. Now, make change and let me take my package of paper and get out of here. I'm sure they're just outside, waiting."

The door closed softly and reopened just as quickly. Al-Hasan came in, alone this time, let the door close on its own, and walked back to the counter.

"I'm sorry, Lissa. I shouldn't have gotten so upset. The money is important to me, but not so I'm angry with you, yes? So now we talk like friends we are. Okay?"

"Yes, okay. But please, can't you just show me something that makes this money yours? I really cannot just hand it over without knowing more. I'd like to know what you do with that much money, and why it can't just be put in your bank account and . . . and well, what makes it such a secret? Why would you have to have it delivered in plastic bags in the park? It just doesn't make sense to me."

"Ah, Lissa. This doesn't have to make sense to you. You only need to know that it is for me, and you need to trust me."

TWENTY-FIVE MINUTES LATER, THE SILVER CAR PULLED TO A STOP in front of the small house. Although David and Rachel Horesh still spoke Arabic at home, it wasn't often that guests or strangers began a conversation in that tongue. The voice of the man at the door was harsh, guttural, and in the old language.

"I must speak with the husband," Dizhwar said, and pushed his way into the small livingroom. "It is about the store."

"David," Rachel called, "A man. Something about the store." She turned again to the intruder, for that is what he was, and tried to control her rising fear. Her mind flashed back to the day more than twenty years before, when other men had pushed into the Horesh compound in Bagdad. Then it had been on orders from the man who still ruled that land; orders to confiscate property and drive out the Jews who foolishly had remained in the country, still believing they would be safe. Suddenly the distance in time and miles didn't seem so great.

David Horesh came into the room, still dressed in his pajamas and robe.

"Yes, the store? What about the store?" His face changed abruptly when he saw Rachel standing in a way that immediately signaled fear. "Rachel? Are you okay?" Then to the man who stood so darkly in his livingroom: "What is the matter at my store? Who are you?"

"Dizhwar is my name, and you must come to your store with me now."

"But why? What had happened? Who are you?"

"Do not delay me. Come now."

"Yes, yes, but what is wrong? I must dress." He turned to walk back to the bedroom. The other man followed him.

"Dress quickly, then. That woman you leave unsupervised in your store has made a big mistake." His voice was quieter, and somehow more sinister now. He stood in the doorway as Horesh pulled a shirt and trousers over his pajamas, slipping his bare feet into soft shoes.

"I still don't understand. Who are you? Is the girl all right?"

213

"No questions. Move!" His hand slipped into his pocket.

"What are you doing to my husband?" Rachel's voice was tense, higher than normal. "You can't just walk in here and order us around. This is not Iraq, this is America."

"Shut up!" Dizhwar turned to Rachel. "I can hurt you if I need to."

David Horesh put a hand out to hold the other man back. "You do not touch my wife, or talk that way to her. I will call the police right now." He turned and reached for the telephone by the bed. The gun came out of Dizhwar's pocket, leveled and aimed at Rachel.

"Pick up the telephone and I shoot. Stop playing. We go now. You too, woman." Gesturing with his gun, he ordered the couple to go through the kitchen into the garage. "You drive. I will sit in back. Remember what I have in my hand."

Still dazed by the last few minutes, the old couple did as they were ordered. In a few minutes they were turning down the side street where the shop stood. David drew up to the curb where an open space was reserved for deliveries. Rachel, her face locked in a blank mask, stared ahead, her heart finally calming, now that they were around other people. From the back seat, Dizhwar ordered the couple to get out, at the same time opening the rear door and stepping onto the sidewalk. "In the store," he ordered, gesturing with his head. David came around the car and took his wife by the hand, leading her as quickly as he could. Rachel tried to hold back, sensing that she was in less danger, perhaps, outside in the open.

Al-Hasan turned quickly as he heard the door open behind him. Lissa involuntarily stepped back, her face impassive, but her mind instantly registered what the arrival of her employer meant.

"What are you doing, Zwani? Why has Mr. Horesh come here?" Behind him she saw Dizhwar, his hand in his jacket pocket. She wished she could stop this performance that the two Iraqis were playing for her benefit, but that wasn't possible. These were desperate men, and she needed to discover what the desperation meant. People were dying; more might die. She didn't stand between them all and death, she knew that. Yet she could not just give in, even if she could not protect David and Rachel.

"You must open your safe, Mr. Horesh. This woman has put something in it that belongs to me." al-Hasan's voice was reasonable with just a hint of menace. He stood back as the old man approached the safe.

"He's right, Mr. Horesch. I'm sorry. I did a stupid thing. But my friend has over-reacted." Lissa's voice was contrite and small. "If you will please open the safe, he will take what is his and leave." The old man did as she asked.

Escorting Lissa to the door, al-Hasan turned back to the bewildered and still angry older couple. Raising the box with the money in it, he smiled. "We have what we want, Jew. Remember we have your girl with us." He nodded to Lissa. "You run your store today. Call no one, and she will come back to you tomorrow. Understand?" The last was spoken in Arabic. David Horesh nodded.

"Now Lissa, you will find out how we will spend our money." With Dizhwar following, the trio got into the Horesh car. "Go back to the house and we'll take our car from there." Dizhwar took the wheel and they were soon at the Horesh home. Leaving the car in the garage, a few minutes later they left by the front door, Lissa in front, Dizhwar following, his hand still in his pocket, and al-Hasan carrying the large cardboard box. The trio drove carefully away from the house, headed out of town. The silver sedan easily blended into the flow of traffic.

STILL UNABLE TO UNDERSTAND all that had happened, David and Rachel stood rooted where they had stood after opening the safe and passing the box to al-Hasan. So disoriented were they that they hardly responded when the door to their office opened and two more strangers walked out. David only turned and took Rachel's hand. They stared at the two men.

"Mr. Horesh, I'm Grady." The gruff voiced man held out his federal identity card. "And this is lieutenant Morris, State Police." He nodded to the man beside him. Stan offered his own ID card. "We will be right behind them. And just to assure you, Ms. King is one of my agents, and fully able to take care of herself." The older couple continued to stand unmoving as the two men passed through the store and out to the street, just in time to see the Horesh car turn the corner. Another car, parked at the end of the block, started and made the same turn.

"Hope your guy knows how to keep out of sight," Grady said.

The two men walked the half-block to the corner, turned and got into Stan's black cruiser. Turning on the electronic systems, Stan adjusted the volume so that they could hear the conversation in the Horesh car.

TAKING LISSA'S SHOULDER BAG FROM HER, Zwani lifted it, weighing it. Handing it back to her, he smiled.

"See how much lighter it is without a great big pistol in it? You know now you don't need that with me, don't you?"

"Are you kidnapping me, Zwani? That's illegal here, you know, regardless of what you can do in your country." She put the bag on the seat between them, comforted by the pressure in the small of her back from the small, ultra-light Beretta tucked into her waistband. His reply, like the rest of their conversation, floated back to Morris's vehicle through the pen-microphone still in the pocket of her bag.

"I'm doing nothing of the kind, Lissa. I am only taking you to show

216

you where our money will be spent, and how it will help bring peace to both our countries."

Back in Morris's car, now several blocks behind them, his radio alerted the two men that the Horesh car was turning into the neighborhood where the owners lived. The tail observed the car going back into the garage as he drove past the house.

"Break off, 245, and we'll track from the radio."

"10-4."

"Lissa dropped a tracker in al-Hasan's car the other night," Stan said. "Slipped it under the seat. We know it's still there."

"Hmpf," was all Grady said in response. "What makes you think they're going to leave the house?"

"They have the money, they're going to do something with it now, and they can't really do it from the house. Anyway, we'll hear what they are saying."

The radio, after the sound of doors opening and closing and footsteps, finally brought some words to the two listeners.

"What are we going to do here, Zwani?"

"Don't ask questions, little girl, just listen." The was the sound of something being moved, a phone number being pressed into a keypad, then his voice again, this time in Arabic. He spoke quickly, hung up the phone and said: "We go now." Again doors opened and closed, an engine started, and the tracker woke up.

"Here we go," Stan said.

The silver car had moved in silence for ten minutes. A mile back, the black cruiser kept pace, Grady following their route on a local area map.

As the car passed a sign indicating they were near an airport, Lissa said: "Bird's Nest Airpark - 1 Mile. Is that where we're going?" She seemed subdued.

"It is where we will go shopping," al-Hasan laughed. "They have something for us to look at."

Dizhwar parked the car next to a large metal building that faced the airfield taxiway. The corrugated sides of the hangar showed age and lack of care. Rust streaks alternated with flat, dirty white paint. Weeds and uncut grass spread out away from the building, giving the whole place a derelict appearance. The three got out of the car and walked into the building.

"Hey!" A tall, thin man in greasy coveralls came from around the other side of the only plane in the hanger. Wiping his hands on his pant legs, he offered a broad smile to the trio.

"Been hoping you were comin' ' back. Just about got the old bird ready for you if you still want it." He gestured toward a Piper Cherokee with the wrench he still held in one hand. The white paint was fresh, and the plane looked much better than its surroundings.

"Yes, we are ready to take it now," al-Hasan said. "We have the money."

"Well, I still have to put the numbers on the tail, and I have one or two things on the engine to adjust. Have it all tomorrow, I guess. Got the airworthiness certificate last week." He gestured toward the office at the side of the hanger. "Come on over here and we can do the paperwork." The trio followed the owner.

"The tanks: they are full?" al-Hasan asked.

"Not yet. I'll see to that when I finish the work."

"We want to take the plane today."

"Well, I can't let you do that, see. New rules. Gotta pass the papers by Washington. But that shouldn't take too long. Where you going to keep it, anyway?"

"I have place, grass field, good hanger. Not far."

"Might as well write it down now. New rules about everything."

"She buying the plane," al-Hasan said, pointing to Lissa. "All in her name."

"You a pilot, miss?"

"No. Just the owner. What do I need to give you?" She opened her bag and brought out her wallet. I don't have a driver's license, but I do have a passport." She handed him the small blue book. "And the address isn't up-to-date. I've been traveling." She smiled what she hoped was a comfortable smile.

"Well, I guess the information I put down will be okay for now. You can always correct it later if you need to. I just need some proof of who you are, and this ought to do." He took the passport and began filling out the form in front of him. "I'll file this for you, and as soon as the okay comes back, the plane is yours. As soon as you pay, of course." He smiled as he looked up. "You be writing a check on a local bank?"

"We pay cash," al-Hasan said. "Like you wanted."

"Whoa! That's the way I like to hear people talk!"

Grady and Stan had parked beside an empty, abandoned gas station just past the turn-off to the air field

"Unless she's in trouble," Grady rumbled, "we'll just see what happens next." The two men sat silently, listening to the conversation still coming in from Lissa's remote microphone.

"I guess that'll be okay, Ms. King." The mechanic handed Lissa her passport. "Now, when you come to pick up the plane, should be tomorrow afternoon, you just go over to the control tower and file a flight plan," he turned to al-Hasan, "and take it away." Zwani nodded. "'Course you might want to just file a test flight before you do that. Give you a chance to make sure it takes off and lands and flies the way you want it. That's what I'd do, anyway."

"We come back tomorrow what time?"

"Oh, anytime after noon, I guess. It's a holiday, but someone will be in the office to take your plan. No later than one o'clock."

"Tomorrow, then."

"I'LL BE FINE, DAVID. My friends apologize for being so high-handed with you and Rachel." The three had returned to the shop, essentially to reassure David and Rachel that she was okay. "I'm so sorry they acted that way, but maybe it was that way for you when you first came here: not always understanding the way we do things. Don't worry." she turned to Zwani: "You just want what's yours, what's coming to you, don't you?" She smiled at her own choice of cliché, and Zwani nodded.

"I think my friend is still afraid," he said. "He was just following my asking him to bring you to help us. I don't expect him to scare you." Dizhwar offered a half-smile of agreement, though Lissa was sure he had known exactly what Zwani had wanted him to do.

David, confident that the men waiting in his office would take care of Lissa, nodded and smiled. "I think I understand. Just take care of my employee. I need her back soon." The two men and Lissa walked confidently out of the shop.

AT LISSA'S APARTMENT, AL-HASAN WAITED and watched while she put a few things into a simple, zippered backpack. Zwani had made it clear that she would be staying the night in his house, to be "ready for the big day tomorrow." As they headed out the door, she picked up what looked like a fishing vest, except that it contained a liner of impact-resistant material. "It can get chilly even in July out in the country," she explained to al-Hasan.

"YOU SLEEP WELL, I THINK?" al-Hasan said as Lissa came into the diningroom the next morning.

"I would have liked to sleep in my own bed, Zwani, but it was okay. I'm sorry that you felt you had to lock the door to the room, though."

Breakfast was served without Dizhwar's help. "He is cleaning up things in the barn," was Zwani's explanation. "We will bring the plane here this afternoon."

MORRIS AND GRADY HAD RETURNED to the closed gas station where they had monitored Lissa's microphone the day before. They had watched as the plane rose up from the airfield, circled, made a few touch-and-go landings and then headed off to the northwest.

"I know where they're going," Stan said. The Piper was in the air, making a slow turn away from the small airfield. "They're headed for the house. That's why the field in front of the barn was so well kept." He started the car. "Take us half an hour to get there. By that time they should be on the ground."

Driving toward the old farm, Stan and Grady said nothing. The microphone in Lissa's purse still carried the conversation that took place as they flew, but the engine noise made understanding difficult.

About ten minutes into the drive the silver sedan, driven by Dizhwar, zipped past the black, unmarked Crown Vic.

"I guess our birds will be flying for a little longer," Grady said. "If you know where they're going, get off this road and maybe stop at a gas station. They can probably see the road."

At a crossroads, Stan turned away from the direction they had been headed. When they got out of the car at a country convenience store they could hear the plane. From the ground they watched as the aircraft grew smaller and smaller. They stood by the car for a few minutes, then went inside the store. Fortified with coffee and what passed for lunch wrapped in plastic, they returned to the car. As they ate, the sound from the aircraft cleared, and they heard Lissa's voice.

"I didn't know you were such good pilot, Zwani. You landed like you had been doing this kind of thing for years."

"In my country I was air force pilot for a few years."

"I thought you had come here to learn to fly. Maybe you just needed to take a refresher course?"

"What's that: 'refresher course'?"

"Getting familiar with something you haven't done for a while."

"Yes. Like that."

The mic now picked up Dizhwar's voice: "When do we do it?"

"When I say so," al-Hasan told him.

"Do what? Are you going to take a trip?"

"Yes, Lissa, we are going to take a trip. The three of us."

"I can't take a trip now. I really have to get back to town and my job."

"No. For now you stay with us. That will be fine. The old man can take care of his business by himself for now."

"But Zwani, I can't just walk out. Besides, I need the job. Especially since you took the money I was hoping to keep."

"Now Lissa, what would you do with all that money? You wouldn't know how to use so much, would you?"

"Why wouldn't I?"

"Girl doesn't need money. That's a man's responsibility: take care of the woman."

Had al-Hasan been paying attention, he might have noticed a sudden tightening of the muscles in Lissa's face. But he wasn't. They were now in the dining room of the old house. The table, no longer set for eating, held instead a roll of maps. As Lissa watched, al-Hasan unrolled them, selected one to spread out, and let the others roll up again.

"Where are we going?" Lissa looked over the man's shoulder. She felt his arm come around her. He put his hand on her back, sliding slowly downward. She turned away from him. "Stop, Zwani. Just tell me where we're going." She had avoided what she knew would be a caress that slipped to her waist, and the small automatic in her waistband.

The man turned to face her. There was a different light in his eyes; a harsh, mean light. "Do not turn away from me, girl. I will decide what we do, and where we do it, and when. You are just along to 'enjoy the ride,' as you Americans like to say."

"We Americans also like to say 'you don't own me,' Zwani. I'm not just an ornament for you to enjoy"

In the listening car, Stan Morris added, "And you'd better not be enjoying at all, my boy." Grady smiled.

"Okay, American girl, we are going to do something very special today. You want to know?"

"Yes, of course I do."

"Then listen to me: we are going to take this airplane you just bought us, and we are going to take a very special trip. We are going to Washington, to see the President."

"And you bought an airplane to do that? I don't think I understand." She did, of course, and so did Stan Morris and Grady and a State Police SWAT unit made up of cops from a regional task force.

"Why would you buy a plane just to do that? It doesn't even take three hours from here by car, and there are airports where you could have rented a plane if you had to fly."

"We are taking your president a special present. That is what Dizhwar is loading right now."

"Zwani," Lissa's voice took on a breathlessness that pretended surprise and shock, "you're going to hurt the president, aren't you? You're planning to fly into the White House, isn't that it?" Her voice quavered.

"Now you are getting smart. And also buying yourself a ticket on this flight." his voice was low and sinister. "Maybe you get too smart."

"But you can't be serious! You'll never get near the place. Oh, Zwani, you can't mean it. You're kidding me. But it isn't nice to make jokes like that."

The man's face darkened, his eyes fierce. "It is no joke, you stupid child. You can't understand, but you will see."

"You know the government will shoot you down if you try to get even close."

"And that's where you come in, you see. On the radio I do not sound American. You will say what I tell you, and by the time they realize what is happening, we will be there."

"No. I can't do it. I won't let you."

"You will stop me?" The man exploded into laughter, grabbed the girl by her arm and pushed her toward the door. "Enough! We are going and you will be with us every second of the way. Now walk!" From the living room it was only ten feet to the front door. Still holding her arm al-Hasan pushed Lissa through the short hallway and out the open front door. "If you try anything, I will have to hurt you, and I don't want to do that."

Lissa stopped and yanked her arm out of Zwani's grip. Facing him, her hands on her hips, she said: "And you don't think forcing me to help you crash into the White House is going to hurt?"

"Lissa, Lissa. Don't fight me. What we are doing will make you a hero for my people; a martyr. You will be admitted to heaven with us!" His eyes were bright with a vision only he could see. Ahead of them the engines of the Cessna began to turn over, cough and fire. The doors to the barn were open, and the plane began to taxi out of the make-shift hanger.

"No, Zwani. Not you, not Dizhwar, not me. None of us are getting off the ground." Her right hand moved to her back, fingers grasped the handle of the small Beretta and pulled it from her waistband. Al-Hasan, not to be thwarted, swung his free hand toward the woman's head. As the gun came forward, Lissa ducked, under his moving arm. Her reflexes, far superior to his, allowed her to bring the gun into position. In the background she heard and felt the engines of the plane rev up to takeoff speed, saw the white fuselage begin to move down the grass runway. A burst of automatic rifle fire accompanied the twisting swerve of the plane as it moved off the runway and sank on one collapsed wheel into the soft earth.

The momentary distraction allowed al-Hasan to move closer to Lissa, to reach out for the still unfired automatic in her hand. As he grasped her wrist, Lissa raised one booted foot, swiftly and accurately connecting with this angry, screaming man; connecting and turning him suddenly pale, connecting and turning him into a crouching, angry but incapacitated animal. Her wrist now freed, she brought the handle of the gun down hard on the man's temple and he toppled to the ground, stunned if not unconscious. Stepping back, holding the gun with both hands, Lissa held her shot and Stan and Grady and the black-clad SWAT team divided and surrounded both al-Hasan and the disabled aircraft.

"The plane has a bomb," Lissa shouted, but the team was already ripping open the cabin door. A very dead Dizhwar rolled out onto the ground. It was a spectacular end to July 4th.

I GUESS," STAN MORRIS SAID, "these guys could fall into the 'dumb crooks' folder." Lissa and Grady and Stan were in the booth at the Pullman Café, slowly working their way through food, beer and an analysis of the events that had brought the three together. "My boss couldn't stop laughing when I told him how you had taken al-Hasan down." Lissa sat back and then leaned against him. "Said he didn't believe these guys were really a threat to national security in the first place."

"You know," Grady spoke with a measure of thoughtfulness he didn't usually display, "even with all the security measures we have in place, and the alert system the Homeland Security folks have set up, there's always a chance that someone will get through, will find a way to bypass the fence or just make such a close call that we could over-react. We can't be everywhere all the time. None of us: not my agency or yours, not the local cops or even the plain old private citizen who keeps his eyes and ears open. We got lucky this time."

"But you knew there was something going on here, didn't you?" Stan turned to Lissa. "You didn't just 'happen' to select this town and the Horesh shop for a vacation." The tone of his voice left a larger question in the air.

"You're still angry about my not telling you, aren't you?" She pulled away just enough to look into his eyes. "I wouldn't have kept it from you if I didn't think it was best, Stan. We," she looked at Grady, "thought that at least until we had something more to go on than a letter, we'd best keep it to ourselves."

"You did that part just fine." Stan sat up straight, turning to look at Lissa. "A letter? You never said anything about a letter."

It was Grady's turn. "About six months ago we had an anonymous letter from here. Turned out to be Horesh himself. He didn't know where to write, so the letter ended up on my desk. I gave it to King because I knew she had lived here, gone to school here, knew the town at least a little."

"When I read the letter I thought it might be from David," Lissa picked up the narrative, " but he had no idea what had happened to me since I graduated. He and Rachel just knew I had gone to Washington for graduate school. It seemed a natural fit for me to at least come down and have a look."

"One of those targets of opportunity we sometimes get," Grady added.

"And what did this anonymous letter have to offer?"

"Only that there were people from Iraq using blind mailboxes in

Beverley, and that the writer thought they might be terrorists. Our analysts felt that the writer was from that region. My first reaction was that whoever wrote the letter was a part of a cell that had been scared off by what the 9-11 people did. Sometimes people do scare themselves off when the chickpeas hit the blender."

"I guess I would have gotten the same message," Stan said reluctantly. "Enough meat in the mix to make you want more."

Alex, the waiter, approached the table. "Another round? How about dessert?"

Waiting for the waiter to return, the conversation shifted slightly. It was Grady who spoke first: "I can't believe how easy it was for you to do what you were doing without making al-Hasan suspicious. How you got away with it, Lissa." he shook his head in mock surprise. "Of course, when you're good, you're good!" He sat back and smiled. "Guess all my lectures paid off somehow."

"That and Zwani's cultural bias," Lissa added.

"Uh, oh," Stan laughed. "I didn't know this was an anthropology exercise, too."

"You know what I mean. Both of you do. These people, people like al-Hasan and Dizhwar and all the rest of 'em can't see me, or any other woman for that matter, through the right lens. They have a built-in reverse telescope."

Stan and Grady exchanged a look that said "soapbox," and let their companion continue.

"If they could see women as people instead of objects, I couldn't have gotten away with it. But think about this: neither of these men could believe that I would be smarter then they were, or stronger, and certainly, not smart enough to see what they were up to. It was really hard for me not to just turn around and knock 'em both to the ground the first time they tried anything."

"Well, yes," Stan mused. "But the first time you went to the house for dinner they slipped you a 'Mickey,' and the next thing you knew, you were in another room, your wire had been discovered, and your gun taken away. Think about what could have happened, Lissa."

"Are you trying to protect me, Stan?" She moved another inch or two away from him, leaning back in what could have been a defensive position.

"Of course I am. Just like I would with Grady or any other partner. Not because I don't think you can handle something. I'm just saying you let yourself get into a really serious position."

"Well, there was a moment when I thought I might have to fight," she said slowly, "but only a moment. And I knew I could if I had to. Anybody can if she's prepared."

"It still comes down to the same thing, Morris," Grady put in. "If you do this kind of work, if you prepare yourself properly, you still have the upper hand. Most of the time."

LISSA TURNED TO FACE THE OTHER PILLOW, empty now but still bearing the impression of Stan's head. She slid her hand under the covers below the pillow, found that it was not still warm, and sat up. As she did, the door opened and with two coffee mugs in one hand, Stan came to her side of the bed.

"I've got my own version of an omelet ready to go when you are," he said, handing her one of the mugs. "But if you don't get a move on there won't be any left."

Lissa sat up, not bothering to cover herself, brought her knees up and sat back against the pillow. Tasting the coffee, she smiled and nodded.

"If the food is as good as the coffee, I'd better not wait." Putting the cup down, she started to slip out of bed.

"Well, I haven't turned on the stove yet."

Lissa raised the coffee mug. "Anything else turned on?"

STANLEY MORRIS AND LISSA KING STROLLED HAND-IN-HAND along one of the winding pathways of Romany Hill Park. Around them walkers, runners, strollers and dogs enjoyed the hot afternoon.

"What are you going to do now, Lissa? I know you aren't going to stay here."

"There's work to do wherever I go, Stan. Grady will have something for me tomorrow. Already intimated that I won't be in the office too long. I don't know what, or where, but there will be something." They stopped under the shade of the trees around the duck pond. Lissa watched a white swan that shared the water as it cruised among the ducks. Putting his hand on her shoulder, Stan turned her to face him.

"Lissa, do you really want to keep being Grady's 'asset?' Could you consider something different?"

"Like what, Stan? Working for Hutcheson? How much more of him can you take?"

"It isn't Hutch I work for, Lissa. You know that. And I know you aren't just working for Grady. I understand about that. No, that's not what I had in mind."

"Then what, Stan? You're proposing that I become your live-in, waiting for you to come home, being domestic? Come on, my love, you can't believe that would work."

"No. I know better than that. I will admit that I have thought about it, wondered what it would be like to have you there with me every day, every night. And then saw us both wondering how we could end even a commitment-lite affair. No. That isn't either of us. I guess I just want to know with some certainty where and when we will meet again."

"That's not possible, is it?" They were standing close, separated only by the space of an emotion. Slowly Lissa looked up into Stan's dark eyes, and their lips met, held and then parted. Stan took a step back, smiled and then walked the curving path away from her.

THE MAN IN THE CELL WAS UNCONSCIOUS, but by the time the medic had run from the hospital to the cell block the prisoner was dead. The machinery of the prison would go to work explaining how a man in isolated, solitary confinement could have assembled what he needed to take his own life, how his removal to the off-shore prison was strictly within the "rules of engagement" where terrorists were involved, and just a hint that he had only been a small part of a much larger story. In the bigger story of those who would destroy our world, Rizwan ibn al-Hasan barely rated a footnote.

S Paul Klein sold his first scripts while still a student at American University, in Washington, D.C. That was the beginning of a successful career as a writer/producer of informational and educational films. He wrote and produced his last script in 2003, for the Corporation for Public Broadcasting. In between were hundreds of produced filmscripts about industry, art, politics, religion, science and medicine.

Now living on a mountain farm in Virginia, Klein has continued writing, focusing on fiction and personal essays. *Accidents of Time and Place,* a novel published in 2007, was a Library of Virginia nominee. *Mixed Freight: Checking Life's Baggage,* is a collection of essays published in 2010. Both are available on Amazon.